The Yellow Sofa

José Maria Eça de Queirós was born in 1843 at Povoa de Varzim in northern Portugal, the son of a local magistrate. He studied law at Coimbra, but came of age intellectually as part of the "generation of 1870," a group of writers, artists, and thinkers concerned with Portugal's future after the 1828-1834 civil war. He entered the diplomatic service before marrying and settling down to the life of a comfortable but committed satirist, dandy, raconteur, and aesthete. He served as consul in Havana, Newcastle, Bristol, and finally Paris, where he died in 1900.

His first writings—travel articles, essays, short stories— were well received by Portuguese critics. But it was his early novels, *The Sin of Father Amaro* (1876) and *Cousin Bazilio* (1878), cast in the naturalism of Zola and Flaubert, that won him recognition on a larger European scale. *The Maias* (1886) confirmed his growing reputation. The voice in these novels is urbane, exact, amused, ironic; but the comedy is tempered by warm sympathy for human frailty and a poignant sense of the fragility of human happiness. His later novels, most notably *The Illustrious House of Ramires* (1900, New Directions Paperbook 785) are set in the countryside, as Eça turned his ironic gaze from the pretentiousness and greed of fashionable society to less familiar targets: liberal reform and the idea of progress itself.

Eça's voice was never easily contained by the realism of his master, Zola. His sensitive wit found perfect foils in both fantasy and satire, making this nineteenth-century master's novels vibrant, various, and still contemporary.

EÇA DE QUEIRÓS

The Yellow Sofa

Translated from the Portuguese by John Vetch

Introduction by José Maria d'Eça de Queirós

A NEW DIRECTIONS CLASSIC

The Yellow Sofa is published by arrangement with Carcanet Press, Ltd., Manchester.

Manufactured in the United States of America
New Directions Books are printed on acid-free paper
First published as New Directions Paperbook 833 in 1996 and reissued as New Directions
Paperbook 1330 in 2016 (ISBN 978-0-8112-2218-1)

Library of Congress Cataloging-in-Publication Data
Queirós, Eça de, 1845-1900.
The yellow sofa / Eça de Queirós; translated by John Vetch
p. cm. — (New Directions)
ISBN 0-8112-1339-0 (alk. Paper)
I. Vetch, John. II. Series.
PQ9261.E3Y45166   1996
869.3'3—dc20   96-23770

10 9 8 7 6 5 4 3 2 1

New Directions Books are published for James Laughlin
by New Directions Publishing Corporation
80 Eighth Avenue, New York 10011

PORTRAIT OF EÇA DE QUEIRÓS
BY RAFAEL BORDALO PINHIERO

The Yellow Sofa

INTRODUCTORY NOTE
by José Maria d'Eça de Queirós

AS I DELIVER THIS VOLUME INTO THE HANDS OF READERS
and critics, I acknowledge disconsolately that I have nothing
to say: this novel has no history, it cannot be explained. It is
not known whence it came, nor at what date. It is not even
known what title the author intended for it. It is anonymous
and unknown. The author never referred to it in any letter,
any conversation, any article; he never offered it to his
publisher, never even mentioned it!

So what can I say in carrying out my task as 'writer of
prologues'? Only what I know. It is very little.

Having cut down the normal pompous 'Introduction'
to the more modest proportions of a 'Note', I have
decided to confine myself to what is necessary to intro-
duce the little volume and to reproduce here—for those
who have not read it—what I have already said in the
introduction to *Capital*.

It came to light one evening at the beginning of the year
1924, in the now famous trunk in which my father's
unpublished manuscripts had been lying for more than a
quarter of a century. There were 115 loose sheets, untitled
and undated, covered with his usual rapid handwriting, and,

as usual, without any polishing up, any correction. From the make-up of the paper, the handwriting, its compactness, especially its subject, I was at first inclined to think that the manuscript had formed part of the broad initial plan for the 'Scenes from Portuguese Life' which would have dated the novel between 1877 and 1889. That, however, was a mere conjecture. Certainly, none of the dozen titles intended for the twelve social – or, more simply, human – studies which were to make up the 'Scenes from Portuguese Life' could reasonably be applied to it.

On the other hand, certain of the novel's characteristics made my conjecture a reasonable one. My father, in a letter to Chardron quoted in the introduction to *Capital*, gave the essential features of the future work, to which he referred as 'A collection of short novels, of no more than 180 to 200 pages, which would be a reflection of contemporary life in Portugal: Lisbon, Oporto, the provinces, politicians, men of affairs, aristocrats, lawyers, doctors, all classes, all manners, would enter into this picture gallery'. And he later added: 'The attraction of these tales is that there are no digressions, no rhetoric, no philosophising: everything is interesting and dramatic, and quickly narrated.' These, in fact, are the features which characterise this novel, which is indeed a brief social study of 200 pages, a picture of the petty bourgeoisie of Lisbon, a short novel in which 'there are no digressions, no rhetoric', and in which 'everything is interesting and dramatic and quickly narrated'.

Later, however, I discovered in another letter, to Luis de Magalhaes, a phrase which left me puzzled. Luis de Magalhaes, then deputy director of the *Portuguese Review*, had sought an unpublished novel by my father for the *Review*; to which my father replied: 'As to the novel, even you cannot realise how long it takes me to work. I have nothing in a drawer ready-made – except a short study which, on account of its rather coarse nature would not suit the *Review*'. The letter was dated from Paris, in 1891.

Could this study of 'a rather coarse nature' that my father did not wish to see published in the *Portuguese Review* be this short novel of such delicate irony, the banal drama which for a while so deeply disturbed the petty lives of Alves and his friend? Did the letter actually refer to the manuscript with which we are now concerned? It is quite possible, the more so in that we hear no more of this study of a 'rather coarse nature', nor is there anything else among my father's papers which can be taken to correspond in any way to this description. And so, as the little study did not suit the *Review*, it doubtless went back into the drawer, where we found it waiting resignedly. However, that too is no more than a conjecture.

But what is the point of piling up hypotheses which no one will ever be able to verify, or arguments which are merely conjectural?

In the end, there are only two points in the confused history of the manuscript which can be asserted with safety and precision: that my father wrote it, and that I have brought it to the light of day.

The first of these points is not open to discussion. It is a fact: it has the indestructibility of a monument from remote Egyptian antiquity.

As for the second, why add comments to justify it here? The book now enters upon its career; at my hands, it comes into the hurly-burly of publication and faces the verdict of criticism. A work of impulse, put on paper with masterly improvisation, it certainly suffers from the deficiencies of a layman's editing—and yet it is with confidence that I place this little book in the hands of the public, certain that the truthfulness of its characters, the intense Lisbon flavour, the charm of its dialogues, the balance of its composition, the irony of its situations—in a word, the consummate art which the manuscript reveals—are the surest guarantee of its success and the best justification for the publicity which I now give it. *Granja*, 1925.

The Yellow Sofa

Translated by John Vetch

I 🎵 ON THAT FATEFUL DAY, GODOFREDO DA CONCEI-
çao Alves, stifled by the heat and out of breath through
rushing from Black Horse Square, pushed open the green
baize door of his office in Gilders Street, precisely when the
wall clock over the bookkeeper's desk was striking two, in that
deep tone to which the low entrance ceiling imparted a
mournful sonority. He paused, checked his own watch,
hanging on a horsehair fob on his white waistcoat, and he did
not conceal a gesture of annoyance at having had his morning
wasted at the offices of the Ministry of Marine. It was always
the same whenever his overseas commission business took
him there. Despite the Director-General's being a cousin of
his, and although he had regularly slipped a silver coin into the
hand of the commissionaire, and had discounted letters of
credit for two minor officials, there was always the same
boring wait to see the Minister, endless turning over of papers,
hold-ups, delays, all the irregular creaking and disjointed
working of an old machine, half falling to pieces.

'Always the same paralysis!' he exclaimed, putting his hat
on the bookkeeper's desk. 'It makes one want to goad them
on like cattle: Hey! Ruço, Hey! Malhado, get on there...'

The bookkeeper smiled. A youth of pale and sickly aspect, he was scattering sand over the broadsheet which he had been writing and said, as he shook it:

'Senhor Machado has left a note in there. It says he is going to the theatre, the Lumiar.'

And as he wiped his brow with his silk handkerchief, Alves concealed a smile behind the handkerchief and began to examine the correspondence, while the bookkeeper went on sprinkling sand.

Outside, for a moment, a wagon shook the narrow street with the clattering noise of horseshoes. Then everything relapsed into an oppressive silence.

Crouched over a packing case, a clerk was printing a name on the lid. The bookkeeper's pen scratched, the clock overhead ticked loudly. And in the extreme heat of the day, the oppressiveness of the low ceilings, a vague odour of rancidity and provisions rose up from the packing cases, the bundles, the dusty pile of pap___.

'Senhor Machado was at the Dona Maria theatre yesterday,' murmured the bookkeeper, as he went on writing.

With a more lively glance and his interest aroused, Alves put down the letter that he was reading.

'What was the play yesterday?'

'*The Snare of Paris*.'

'What did you think of it?'

The bookkeeper looked up from the letter to reply:

'I liked Teodorico very much...'

Alves was expecting more details, an appreciation. But, as the bookkeeper had again taken up his pen, he continued with his reading. For a moment, the task of the crouching clerk caught his attention. He followed the brush, admiring the curves of the letters.

'Give him a *tilde* accent! Fabião has a *tilde* . . .'

And the clerk was momentarily embarrassed, as Alves stooped down, took the brush and gave Fabião his accent.

He then gave some further instructions to the bookkeeper concerning an order for red felt for Luanda; and pushing open another green door, went down two steps – on that mezzanine floor the levels differed – and going into his own office, he could at last unbutton his waistcoat and stretch out in the green repp chair.

Outdoors, the July day was sweltering, scorching the paving stones; but here in the office where the sun never penetrated, in the shadow of the high buildings opposite, there was coolness; the green blinds were drawn, making it shady; and the varnish of the two desks – his own and his colleague's – the rug that covered the floor, the well-brushed green repp of the armchairs, a gilt moulding which framed a view of Luanda, the glaze of a large wall map – everything had an air of tidiness, of orderliness, which made things restful and cooler. There was even a bunch of flowers which his wife, the excellent Lulu, had sent him the previous day, her feelings stirred by knowing that, on a sultry morning, in the oppressiveness of an office, he lacked the bright colour of a flower to gladden his eyes. He had put the bouquet on Machado's desk; but, lacking water, the flowers were withering.

The green door opened to reveal the bookkeeper's pale unhealthy face:

'Did Senhor Machado leave any instructions about the Colares wine for Cape Verde?'

Alves then remembered his colleague's note, lying on a scribbling pad. He opened it; the first two lines explained about his visit to the Lumiar, then it went on 'As regards the Colares ...' Alves gave the note to the bookkeeper and when the door closed again, he smiled the same smile as before, but now he did not hide it. Since the month began, this was the fourth or fifth time that Machado had disappeared from the office like this, now to go to the Lumiar to see his mother, then in the opposite direction to visit a consumptive friend, and yet again with no explanation or just a few vague words, 'a little business matter'. And Alves smiled. He well understood that 'little business matter'.

Machado was twenty-six and a handsome fellow. With his blond moustache, wavy hair and elegant manner, the ladies liked him. Since they had become partners, Alves knew him to have had three affairs: a beautiful Spanish girl, infatuated with him, had left her rich Brazilian, an influential former provincial president, who had set her up in a house; then an actress from the Dona Maria theatre who possessed little beyond her beautiful eyes; and now this 'little business matter'. But this new affair must be more delicate, occupying a more important place in Machado's heart and life. Alves was well aware of a certain restless and preoccupied air on his colleague's part, perhaps of self-consciousness, at times of sadness. Yet Machado had never told him anything about his exploits, never shown the least inclination to open up and confide in him... They were close friends, Machado spent many evenings at Alves' home, treated Lulu almost as a sister, dined there every Sunday; yet, either because he had come into the business only three years before, or because he was ten years younger, or because Alves had been one of his father's friends and executors, or even because he was a married man, Machado maintained towards him a certain reserve, a vague respect, and there had never been established between them a real male comradeship. Nor had Alves ever referred to any of it. The 'little matter' was nothing to do with the business of the firm, nor was it any business of his.

Despite these repeated absences, Machado continued to be very hard-working, stuck to his desk for ten or twelve hours on steamship sailing days—active, shrewd, living entirely for the prosperity of the firm. And Alves could not but admit that if, in the business, he himself stood for good conduct, domestic honesty, a regular life, sobriety of habits, then Machado provided the commercial shrewdness, energy, decisiveness, broad ideas, the business flair.

He, Alves, had always been naturally indolent, like his father, who chose to move from room to room in a wheeled chair.

Yet, despite his strong principles – of a boy strictly educated by the Jesuits, full of proper beliefs – and one who had never before his marriage had a single adventure or illicit love affair, he nevertheless felt a vague and indulgent sympathy with those 'affairs' of Machado's. First, on account of friendship – he had known Machado as a little boy, pretty as a cherub. Then, his colleague's good family had never ceased to impress him – his uncle, the Viscount of Vilar, his society connections, the fuss that Dona Maria Forbes made of him when she invited him to her Thursdays, despite his being in commerce. He admired the man's good manners and certain elegant refinements; and he was depressed by his own inability to keep up with Machado's air of distinction. And there was another reason, one of temperament, why despite himself he did not cease to sympathise with Machado's amorous affairs. It was because, at bottom, this man of thirty-seven, already rather bald, with a full black moustache, was still something of a romantic. He had inherited this from his mother, a skinny lady who played the harp and spent her time reading poetry. She it was who had given him that ridiculous name, Godofredo. Later on, the sentimentality which she had for many years devoted to literary matters, to moonlight, to romantic love affairs, was turned towards religion; with the onset of religious mania, this reader of Lamartine became a fanatical follower of the Lord; it was then that she had decided to have him educated by the Jesuits and her last days had been a perpetual fear of Hell. From her he had inherited something of all this. As a boy, he had all sorts of crazes which did not last, wavering between the poetry of Garrett and the Sacred Heart of Jesus. After an attack of typhoid fever, he calmed down; and when the opportunity arose to take over his uncle's commission business, he was practical and faced up to life in its material and serious aspects. Yet, in his soul, there remained a vague romanticism which was not disposed to die. He was fond of the theatre, of melodramas, of violent events. He read a lot of novels; great deeds and grand passions excited him. He sometimes felt himself capable of heroism or tragedy. But all this was vague, almost subconscious, silently stirring in his inmost heart. Above all, romantic love affairs interested him, but he never thought of actually experiencing their sweetness or their bitterness. He was a virtuous man who loved his Lulu … but he enjoyed seeing these things in the theatre or reading about them. And now, the romance which he detected by his side, in his own office, interested him. It was as though the merchandise, the mass of paper, had been enlivened by that vague odour of romance emanating from Machado.

Again the door opened and the bookkeeper's wan countenance appeared. He had come to return Senhor Machado's note and before he withdrew, he said through the half-open door:

'The annual general meeting of the Transtagana Company is today.'

Alves was somewhat startled.

'But it's held on the ninth of the month!'

'Today is the ninth.'

Of course, he was well aware that it was the ninth. But the thought of the annual meeting of the Transtagana had reminded him sharply of his wedding anniversary. In the first two years, it had been a day for an intimate celebration, a pleasant dinner with the family, a little dancing in the evening to the sound of a simple piano. After that, the third anniversary had coincided with the early days of mourning for his mother-in-law, the house still melancholy and Lulu in tears. And now this festive day was passing, almost over, and neither of them had remembered. Lulu certainly had not remembered. When he had left home that morning, she had been doing her hair and had said nothing to him. It would be a pity for that auspicious day to pass without a bottle of port being drunk, with a special sweet for dessert. Moreover, his father-in-law and sister-in-law should have been invited, especially as their good relationship had cooled recently, an estrangement on account of a new maidservant who was dominating the widower's household. After all, on such a day, as on a birthday, such matters were forgotten, family feeling holding sway. And he decided to go home at once to São Bento Street, to remind Lulu of the important date, and to send a greeting to his father-in-law who was living at Santa Isabel. It was almost three o'clock, the letters had been signed, there was no more business to attend to that day in the lull which invariably followed the turmoil of the steam-ship for Africa. So he took up his hat and rejoiced in the half-holiday, which gave him the happy idea of going and surprising his darling Lulu with a warm embrace. Normally, that would happen only after half past four, when the office closed. Only one thing disappointed him, that Machado was at the Lumiar and would not be able to dine with them.

'Will you be back?' asked the bookkeeper, noticing that he had put on his hat.

For a moment, Alves thought of inviting the bookkeeper, but he feared that Machado might be offended at knowing that his place had been so easily filled.

'I won't be back. If Senhor Machado should by any chance come in – it's unlikely – but if he does, we are expecting him at seven, as arranged.'

As he went down the steps, he felt as happy as if he had just been married. With the heat, he had an intense longing to go home, to put on his linen jacket and slippers and stay there, waiting for dinner, enjoying his own place, the movement and company of his lovely Lulu. And in the wave of happiness that swept over him, he had a bright idea – to take Lulu a present. He thought about a fan and then decided on a bracelet that he had seen in a jeweller's shop window a few days earlier: a golden serpent with two rubies for eyes, biting its own tail. And this present had a special significance: the serpent symbolised lasting continuity, the sequence of happy days, something that goes on endlessly turning in a golden circle.

His only fear was that the trinket would be too expensive. But no, only a fiver, and as he examined it, the jeweller told him that he had just sold another such to the Marchesa de Lima. He hesitated no longer but paid at once and when he had gone a few paces down the street, he stopped at a shady spot, opened the box and gave it another look, so pleased was he with his purchase. And as so often happens to someone giving a present, he was overcome by emotion . . . like a door opening into a man's egoism and innate greed, and through it a broad tide of latent generosity sweeping in. At that moment, he would have liked to be rich, so as to be able to give her a diamond necklace. For she deserved it. They had been married four years and never had there been a cloud between them.

The moment he had first seen her, one evening in Pedrouças, he had worshipped her; but he could now admit that he had at first been overawed by her. He had thought her proud, exacting, aloof. All because of her lovely figure, her big dark eyes, her erect bearing, her crisp wavy hair...But in that magnificent body of a barbarous queen, he had discovered the heart of a child. She was good, charitable, light-hearted, and her disposition was as placid and gentle as the limpid surface of a summer river.

Some four months ago, for a brief while, she had shown some depression, a little melancholy, a touch of nerves, so that he had wondered whether . . . But unfortunately, it was not that! It had been nerves. It had passed and a reaction followed – never had she been more tender, so happy as in the recent past, filling him with such contentment.

And beneath his sunshade in the burning heat, as he climbed up New Street at Carmo, all this was dancing merrily in his heart. At the top of the street, at Mata's restaurant, he stopped to order a fish pie for six o'clock. He also bought a cold ham and looked around to see what else he could take, eager and happy as a bird that is furnishing its nest. Then he climbed the Chiado. He stopped for a moment to look at a poet and historian, a celebrity, who wore an old silk jacket and straw hat and was at that moment chatting at the entrance of the Bernard, about to blow his nose with his enormous flowered handkerchief. Alves admired his novels and liked his style. He then bought some cigars for his father-in-law, for after dinner. Finally, he went down the Post Office steps which glittered in the sunlight, dusty and dry. In spite of the heat, he walked quickly, fingering from time to time the box with the bracelet, which he had put into his jacket pocket.

He had reached São Bento Street, a few steps from home, when he saw their servant girl, Margarida, waiting at the confectioner's counter. He at once realised that Lulu had not forgotten the happy date, their anniversary; Margarida had been sent to buy cakes and pastries.

In a couple of paces, he entered his own door. It was a building of two storeys, painted blue, hemmed in between two tall buildings. He occupied the first floor, and was not on good terms with his neighbours above—noisy, common people—and did not like their sharing the comfort he had brought into the entrance hall, when at Lulu's request he had had the staircase carpeted. But he had not regretted it; it was always a pleasure, on entering the building, to feel beneath his feet the carpet covering the stairs, giving him a feeling of solid comfort. All this helped his self-esteem.

Upstairs, the maid Margarida had just returned and left the door ajar; deep silence reigned within the house; everything seemed to be asleep in the extreme heat of the day. A strong glare came from the skylight, and the bell-pull, with its scarlet tassel, hung motionless.

Then he had an absurd idea, like a playful bridegroom—to go, step by step, into the lounge and surprise Lulu, who at that hour would normally be dressing for dinner. And he was already smiling at the little cry that she would give, perhaps in her white skirt, her lovely arms bare ... The first room was the dining-room which led, through two curtained doors, to her boudoir and the drawing-room. He went in. On the carpeted floor, his light summer shoes made not the slightest sound. Everything seemed deserted, in a silence so complete that he could even hear the sound of frying coming from the kitchen and the canary hopping about in its cage on the balcony. He went towards the boudoir curtain and, smiling a little smile, was going to draw it and surprise her, when there came from behind the half-drawn curtain of the drawing-room a slight noise, indistinct, something of a sigh, a throat being cleared.

18 *The Yellow Sofa*

Hearing her there, he turned, peeped in...And what he saw – good God! – left him petrified, breathless. The blood rushed to his head and so sharp was the pain at his heart that it almost threw him to the ground. On the yellow damask sofa, fronting a little table on which there stood a bottle of port, Lulu in a white negligee, was leaning in abandon on the shoulder of a man whose arm was around her waist, and smiling as she gazed languorously at him.

The man was Machado!

2 𝕱 AS THE CURTAIN MOVED, LUDOVINA HAD SEEN him, and with a cry, instinctively jumped up from the sofa. Alves heard the cry but was quite unable to move. He found himself slumped, he knew not how, in a chair beside the door and he was trembling, cold all over, yet shaking as in a fever. Through the tumult of the fever, which filled his head and left him bereft of thought, he heard the turmoil going on in the drawing-room, heavy footsteps pacing the carpet, whispered words anxiously exchanged... There was the sound of the latch on the door leading to the staircase, then silence. Then the thought that the two of them had fled restored his strength, anger possessed him, and with a leap he burst headlong into the room. But he stumbled over a fox skin which adorned the doorway and went sprawling ridiculously on the carpet. When he got to his feet, his fists clenched in fury, the curtain at the door to the staircase was swinging to and fro in the breeze: there was no one in the room.

The Yellow Sofa 19

He ran to the landing; with its refined air of middle-class respectability, the staircase descended beneath the bright glare of the skylight. Then he dashed wildly to the window. Along the street outside, with cowardly steps, Machado was taking himself off, his sunshade in his hand. So where was she? Turning round, he saw the maid, Margarida, in the middle of the room, bewildered, with the box of cakes in her hand.

'Where is she?' shouted Alves.

At first, the poor creature did not understand, but suddenly she dropped the box, lifted her apron to her eyes and burst into tears. He thrust her away, almost threw her to the floor, and ran to the kitchen. With the door closed, the cook, singing loudly as she scaled the fish, had heard nothing, knew nothing. So Alves threw himself against the door of Ludovina's room. It was locked.

'Open, or I'll break in!' he cried.

There was no reply. He put his ear to the door panel; from inside came a quiet sobbing, a murmur of anguish and terror.

'Open or I'll break in!' he shouted again. Filled with thoughts of bloodshed and death, he threw a punch at the door, as though he were beating her.

From within, a distressed voice answered with a beseeching cry:

'But do not hurt me!'

'I swear that I will do you no harm...Open! Open!'

The key turned. He burst in; Ludovina, in her magnificent white peignoir, took refuge behind the bed, wringing her hands, her eyes wide open with fear and full of tears.

And then, face to face with the sobbing woman, his anger abated, he stood there, his throat constricted, staring madly at her and almost weeping too. She took two slow paces towards him, her arms outstretched, and her voice – her whole being – trembled as she cried out, through her tears:

'Oh, Godofredo, for your own sake, forgive me. I have done no harm, and it was only the first time …'

His voice choking, he could only mutter through clenched teeth:

'The first time … The first time …'

His rage increased, burst out in a roar:

'And even if it were the first time, why should there be a first time? What infamous behaviour – and with *him*! I ought to have killed you! Go away, get out of here, leave me, you creature! Go away, go away!'

She left the room, weeping desperately. Then, turning round, Alves noticed the cook at the door into the passage, peering inquisitively, excitedly, and behind her, more in the shadow of the corridor, Margarida, upset and cowering, but peeping nevertheless.

'What are you two doing here?' he shouted. 'Get back to the kitchen! One sound from you and you're both out!'

And he slammed the door, went on furiously pacing the room, where the double bed, with its pillows side by side, showed its whiteness. And through the blood that was pounding in his head his thoughts were beginning to sort themselves out. He decided to fight Machado in a duel to the death; and, as for her, to send her home to her father. He also considered sending her to a convent, but it seemed more dignified for himself, more degrading for her, to go and hand her back to her father. When he had weighed things up, and decided on these two resolves, his extreme rage subsided.

Now, with his hard and sombre feeling of grief was mingled the need – imperative, cold and penetrating – to avenge himself . . . And the house seemed once more to be sleeping in the sun, holding in its atmosphere only the silent heat of the anger that had passed.

In front of his mirror, Alves tried to compose his appearance, even adjusted his cravat, and pushed open the door into the dining-room. There she was, sitting in a chair against the wall, her handkerchief in her hand, weeping softly and, between the tears, blowing her nose. Her lovely black hair was still held in a red hair net, and her negligee which she had loosened showed a touch of the lace of her bodice, a hint of the whiteness of her bosom. He did not like to see her weeping. Cold and hard, he looked towards the window, as he said:

'Get your things ready to go home to your father's.'

Keeping his eyes turned towards the window, he noticed that the gentle weeping behind him had stopped, but she did not answer him. He was waiting for an appeal, a cry of friendship, a word of regret: but all he heard was the blowing of her nose. So again he turned more aggressive.

'In my house,' he went on, still facing the window and in a biting tone that ought to have burned her up, 'I want no prostitutes. You can take everything... Take away everything that is yours. But get out!'

He turned away, went and locked himself in his study, a sort of small recess in which there was only a desk and a bookcase. He sat down, took out a sheet of paper, put the date at the top, his hand trembling and making his fine business handwriting shaky. He was in doubt whether he ought to say 'My dear Papa' or merely 'Dear Sir' and he decided on the latter form, for their whole relationship was now at an end; now he had no family. And faced by the blank white sheet of paper, he went on thinking, turning over in his mind the thought—now he had no family. Deep sadness seized him, an immense feeling of self-pity. Why had this happened to him—so decent, so hard-working, so much in love with her? His eyes filled with tears. But he did not want to upset himself, he wanted to write his letter coolly and quickly. Yet, as he pulled out his handkerchief to wipe his eyes, he came upon a box, the box with the bracelet! He opened it and for a moment examined it in its silken nest, the golden serpent with its ruby eyes, winding itself round, biting its tail. So this was the beautiful symbol of the eternal succession of happy days, one following the other like an endless golden circle. He felt a burning desire to humiliate her, to throw in her face all his acts of kindness, his sacrifices, the trinkets he had given her, and extravagances—the box at the São Carlos, and the dedication of his love. Unable to contain himself, he went back to the dining-room, his lips loaded with accusations. She was still there, but on her feet now, wiping her eyes and gazing blankly at the building opposite, as he had done. Her lovely profile was suffused with light and the soft line of her dress emphasised the gracefulness of her figure. At once, he felt that words were drying up in his mouth.

He could find no opening for his strictures and, at the other window, furiously twirled his moustache, his heart in torment and his lips unable to utter a word. At last, an absurd idea came out of his romantic indecision. He threw the bracelet on to the table and exclaimed:

'Put that in your suitcase, too: I bought it for you today, it is yet another present...'

Instinctively she glanced at the bracelet box. Then she began to weep again. These silent tears annoyed him, unnerved him:

'Why do you keep on crying? Whose fault is it? It isn't mine, for I have never denied you anything.'

Then there was a scene. As he paced about the room, he cast up at her, in a quick low voice, all his tenderness, all his devotion. She lowered herself into a chair, weeping all the while; it seemed that she must go on for ever weeping like that.

'Oh, do stop weeping,' he exclaimed. 'Say something, explain... Have you nothing to say by way of excuse? Was it you who sought all this, was it you who provoked him?...'

Still seated, she quickly looked up. Through her tears, a light shone in her eyes, and eagerly, like someone putting out a hand to avoid falling, she blamed Machado. It had been he, he alone had been to blame. It had all begun four months earlier, when Godofredo had taken her to the Dona Maria. And Machado had begun it, talking to her, tempting her and writing to her; he would turn up when Godofredo was at the office, and one day, in the end, almost by force...

'I swear to you that was how it was...I did not seek it, I always pleaded with him...Then I was afraid that Margarida would hear the noise...'

Alves listened to all this, his face livid.

'Let me see his letters,' he said at last, in a voice that was barely audible.

'I haven't got them...'

He took a step across the room, saying 'I shall find them.'

She got up with a cry, putting her arms round him. 'I swear I haven't got them. As God may save me, I gave them all back to him, days ago.'

He pushed her to one side, went to the dressing-table. As it happened, the bunch of keys was on the marble top, among the little bottles. And he began a frantic search among the handkerchiefs, the lace, the boxes of fans, a woman's personal things. Repeatedly she clutched his arm, swore to him that she had no letters. But he silently persisted, pushing her away and ransacking the drawer. An ivory fan broke in pieces as it fell; the beads of a rosary, with its crucifix, lay on the floor.

And just when it seemed that she was telling him the truth, he saw the bundle of letters, tied with a silk ribbon, between two brushes and foolishly exposed to his gaze right from the start. He tore the bundle apart, separated them; they were not from him. The first he opened began: 'My angel'. He put them quietly in his pocket, turned towards her as she remained prostrate at the bedside and said:

'Get ready to go this very day.'

He went back to his study, and there he read the letters, one by one. Nothing could have been more fatuous, with the continual repetition of conventional and banal expressions: 'My beloved angel, why did not God arrange that we should meet long ago?' 'My love, do you realise that I would give my life for you?' And even: 'Oh, that I might have been allowed to bear your son . . .'

And every phrase smote his heart like a silent blow that knocked him out. One in particular infuriated him, as it began: 'My soul's darling, what an afternoon that was yesterday . . .'

So then, his pen almost tearing the paper, he quickly wrote the letter to his father-in-law, a few simple words – that he had found his wife with a man, and wished him to come and get her, take her away. Otherwise, he would put her out of the house like a whore, indifferent to what fate might befall her. In a postscript, he added that he would be going out between five and seven – so asked him to take advantage of this absence and come and get his daughter. He put the letter in his pocket, buttoned his jacket, rubbed his silk hat on his sleeve and went out.

On the staircase, he met a youth in a white apron, with a basket on his arm.

'Is this where Senhor Alves lives?'

It was the pie, the ham, the country cheese – all the good things he had bought. A spasm of grief gripped his heart. He had to hold on to the banister to avoid falling. The youth looked at him in astonishment.

'Is it from Mata's?'

'Yes, sir,' replied the youth, terrified by this gentleman who seemed so unwell.

Godofredo murmured 'Go up and knock.' And he stood listening. He heard the youth ring, the door open, then Margarida's voice from within, saying:

'It's a boy bringing a pie, madam.'

He went down the stairs four at a time – but down below, remembering the deep decorum of the staircase, he tried to calm down, buttoned up his jacket, passed his hands over his face, got ready to pass his neighbours, and went out, with that air of solid prosperity which had made him so much respected in the neighbourhood.

3 🦶 BY GOOD FORTUNE, AT THE DOOR OF THE NEARBY grocer's shop stood a Galician who sometimes ran errands for him and knew his father-in-law's house. He handed him the

letter, telling him to deliver it in person and not to wait for a reply. And as he knew the good reputation of the grey-haired Galician in his service to the neighbourhood, he added:

'Take care, in your own hand, there's money in it ... a bank note.'

The old man put the letter inside his shirt, next to his heart.

And then Alves set himself, at a distance, to track the letter. He watched the man go into his father-in-law's apartment, a shabby four-storey tenement, with a second-hand shop beneath it. Neto lived at the top, with a balcony on which there stood a bowl of flowers. For an eternity, he went on watching the entrance from a distance. But the Galician did not come down and he began to fear that his father-in-law might not be at home. If he were to return later, after dining out, there would be no sign of him until late at night. In that event, what ought he to do? Roam the streets in the hope that his wife would have departed? This thought gave him an awful feeling of desolation and confusion, as though the proper order of things had come to an end for ever. Suddenly, he saw the Galician; he had handed over the letter to Senhor Neto, and immediately come down, without waiting. Feeling relieved, Alves went on walking aimlessly; and bit by bit his steps took him by the daily route towards his office. He went down the Chiado; in Gold Street, he paused for a moment to look at a pistol in the Lebreton shop window, and the thought of death crossed his mind. But he did not want to think about that now, nor about his duel. Soon, when he went home at seven o'clock and found the place empty, he would certainly think about the duel, about settling accounts with the other man. So he went on walking, aimlessly. For a moment he considered going to the Public Promenade, but he was fearful of meeting Machado there. He went through Black Horse Square, along the Aterro, almost as far as Alcantara. He moved like a sleep-walker, noticing neither the people who jostled him nor the beauty of the summer evening, dying in the splendour of living gold. He was thinking of nothing in particular, in his mind there was a jumble of ideas, with all manner of things passing through it – memories of his courtship of Ludovina, days taking walks with her, but then ... the way she had been lying with that man's arm around her and the port wine before them! Insistently, bits of her letters came back to him – 'My angel, why shouldn't I have had a child by you?' That was precisely what she had said to himself, at night, in the warmth of their bed, with their lips together. Now he was glad not to have had a son from that shameless woman!

It got darker; he considered going home. Extreme fatigue gripped him, brought on by the extreme excitement, the long walk in the sultry air of the July day. He went into a café, drank a large glass of water, and stayed seated with his head resting against the wall, surrendering to the pleasure of his brief rest in semi-shade.

Warm twilight enveloped the city. After the day's extreme heat, all the open windows were inhaling the air, one after another lights were coming on, people were to be seen passing by, overcome by the heat, hat in hand. And he had a small feeling of pleasure in the shade and restfulness; it seemed that his pain was lessening, dissolving in his bodily inactivity, in the shadows of nightfall. And there came over him a wish to stay there for ever, with the lights unlit, never needing to move or take a single step. The thought of death took hold of him, tranquil and insinuating, like a caressing breath. He truly wanted to die. In the state of collapse into which his body had fallen, all the bitter experiences which he must yet endure – the cruelties that he had had to suffer, the return to the lonely house, the encounter with Machado, the steps to be taken in arranging for seconds – all seemed like giant forces, intolerable rocks which his feeble hands would never be able to lift. It would be delightful to lean his head against that wall, to stay there on that bench – dead, liberated, freed from pain, having departed from life like the peaceful silence of a light extinguished. For a moment, he thought about suicide. The idea of killing himself did not terrify him or make him tremble. But to search for a weapon, to move a step and throw himself into the river, such steps would be repugnant to him in the complete failure of his willpower. He would have liked to die where he was, without moving. If a word, an order given within himself, would suffice to put an end to him, he would calmly say that word ... And perhaps *she* would weep, perhaps feel his loss ... But what about the other man?

At that thought, his resolve returned – a flicker of energy, still faint, yet sufficient to allow him to get up, go on with his walk. Yes, Machado would be content if he were to disappear for ever, that very night. His feeling would be one of complete relief! For a day or so, he might behave as though he felt sorry, might even really feel upset. But then his life would go on; the firm would become Machado & Co. Machado would go on having other mistresses, go to the theatre and wax his moustache ... That was it! It was the other who had caused the destruction of a beautiful happiness, he was the one who ought to die. It was Machado who ought to disappear, Machado who ought to be killed. That indeed would be more just.

And then matters would be different; the firm would go on being Alves & Co., later he would be reconciled with his wife and life would continue, peaceful and calm ... That was how it ought to be. If God looked first at one, then the other, weighing up the merits and the faults of each, He ought to make Machado disappear, inspire in *him* the thought of suicide!

And so, out of these absurd fancies, balancing each other in his troubled spirit – his own suicide, the suicide of the other man – an idea emerged, like a lightning flash between two dark clouds, clear in all its details, an idea that seemed just, attainable, the most appropriate, the only worthwhile course: to put it to Machado that one of them should commit suicide!

At that moment, something familiar about the houses past which he was walking made him realise that he had unthinkingly come back to his own door. Entirely absorbed with the thought of Ludovina, he stopped and stared at the house. With the gas lamp in front, the clean respectability of its blue-painted façade made a break between two tall buildings. On his own floor, all was shut up, in darkness behind green venetian blinds. Would she still be there? Would her father have come and fetched her? And a dreadful worry made his heart beat quickly. For an instant, he wanted her to be there, he thought of forgiveness, so much did the sight of those blind windows terrify him. And yet he felt that, confronting her, he would be cold, constrained . . . No, it would be better if they never saw each other again!

Curiosity then drew him to his father-in-law's house, at the end of the street. There the tall building stood, neglected, dirty. On the third floor, his father-in-law's, the open windows were drawing in the coolness of the evening, but no light was to be seen. Neither of the silent façades gave him any answer or took away his dreadful feeling of unease.

He went back home, pushed open the door. The carpeted staircase was asleep under the warm light of the gas lamp, and the muffled sound of his own steps seemed to echo through a deserted, hollow place. From the upper floor came the sound of a piano, sounding solemn, something from *Faust*. The people up above were happy, they were playing the piano!

The cook came to open the door and at once something in her manner told him that Ludovina had gone. In the dining-room, on the oiled tablecloth, a candle was burning. He took it and went into the bedroom. At once he noticed the locked suitcase and the trunk. But around the room there were still things of hers: by the bed were her slippers and spread out over the chaise-longue the white negligee she had worn that morning. And other things had been left: glass bottles on the dressing-table, and a wooden image of the Virgin to which she was greatly attached.

He put down the candle on the dressing-table and saw his own face reflected in the mirror—pale, haggard, staring at him with a look of devastation and abandon.

Uncertainly, he took up the candle and went into the drawing-room. There was still the appearance of disaster; the fox skin rolled to one side; on the table, opposite the sofa, the bottle of port; and on the edge of a plate, the stub of Machado's cigar. Faced with that cigar end, a deep anger seized him. He felt as though he was being battered by a strong iron fist. He shuddered as though from a deep insult and swore that he would be iron-hard, unforgiving, that he would himself send the luggage away, and would see the other man dead at his feet . . . or die himself!

Nevertheless, he forthwith decided to resist that disturbed, anxious feeling. He wanted orderliness to hold sway in his spirit, everything in the house to resume its air of regularity and calmness. She had gone; her luggage should go after her, that very night! Henceforth, he would be a widower, yet the routine of the household would continue, without disorder, serenely.

Quickly he called out for Margarida: 'Well, is no one to dine in this house today? Time is getting on but the table is not laid!'

The creature looked at him as though astounded that he should want to have dinner at home, should have returned to dine. She was certainly about to say something in reply, but he glared at her and she sidled out, crestfallen, and within a few moments she laid the table, making haste, showing her zeal, as though she wanted to make amends for her slight complicity; and she put on the table everything that the basket had contained – the pasty, the ham, the country cheese...

Meanwhile Alves went to his study. The idea that had suddenly possessed him as he was returning from his miserable ramble – the solution which seemed the only one possible – came back to him, establishing itself in his mind and becoming the centre of his whole activity. It was very simple: they would draw lots, he and the other one, to decide which of them should kill himself! Nor did this seem to him far-fetched or tragic or extravagant; on the contrary, it was the rational, honourable course and the only practical one. He felt sure he was thinking things out very coolly. A duel with swords, two shirt-sleeved business men aiming clumsy and futile thrusts at each other until one was wounded in the arm – that seemed to him ridiculous; nor was it fitting that they

34 *The Yellow Sofa*

should exchange a couple of pistol shots, miss each other, and then each of them, flanked by his seconds, turn and climb ceremoniously into hired carriages. No! for an outrage such as this, death alone; just a single loaded pistol, drawn by lots between them, and fired at a handkerchief's distance. Yet he doubted whether this was really possible. Where would they find sponsors who would agree, be willing to share in the responsibility for the tragedy? In vain would he explain the offence to them: to a husband, unfaithfulness is a serious matter, but other people would regard it as a mere misfortune, not calling for such bloody excesses. Besides, if he himself were the one to die, well and good, that would be the end of it, but if he were to see the other man fall down at his feet, what kind of existence would his be afterwards? He would have to flee, abandon his business, seek his fortune afresh in a foreign land, but where? And the great problem still remained: where would be the sponsors for such a course? Moreover, there would be scandal, gossip. the whole truth would come out. Whereas, by the other course everything would be easy, secret, respectable, without inconveniencing anyone; they would draw lots and the one who lost would have to kill himself within a year! If he were the one to lose, he would not hesitate a moment, he would kill himself at once – and he did not doubt that Machado would agree. How could he refuse? He had dishonoured him, he ought to pay with his life ... All the same, he had an uneasy foreboding that he himself would be the loser ...

'If *he* were to meet his end, so much the better,' he thought.

What pleasure could life now bring him, in that lonely house, always on his own, without even the enjoyment of work remaining to him, for he had lost the zest for doing it.

He hesitated no longer. He at once wrote a curt letter to Machado, asking him to be at the office next day, Sunday, at ten o'clock...He was sealing the letter when Margarida came to tell him that dinner was on the table. He hurriedly picked up his hat, went down into the street, left the letter in the postbox by the grocer's and returned to the dining-room, while Margarida and the cook, with the soup tureen getting cold, were astonished at their master's strange behaviour.

The maid's presence embarrassed him. He felt her to be an accomplice in the disgraceful business. For a moment, he thought of dismissing her. But that would only be to loosen her menial tongue in other houses, recounting his fate and discussing his misfortune. He preferred to hold on to her, to put up with her presence, so as to maintain her silence, through her fear of being dismissed.

He had unfolded his napkin, taken up the soup tureen, when the doorbell rang violently.

Margarida went to the door, while Alves remained in suspense, his heart pounding...The girl came running back and in a voice with which she might have announced the appearance of avenging and retributive Providence, exclaimed:

'It is Senhor Neto, sir.'

4 ⚓ NETO CAME IN. SEEING THE TABLE LAID — THE LARGE
pasty and the ham, and Alves with his napkin tucked into his
collar and the bottle beside him – Neto paused at the door, his
hat in one hand, his cane in the other, his eyebrows raised in
surprise. At last, with a touch of sarcasm, he muttered:

'Well, I see you've not lost your appetite!'

Alves at once stood up, took a candle from the sideboard
and moved towards the drawing-room. But Neto protested:

'No, sir, we have time to talk, finish your dinner...'

Alves, however, after lifting a spoonful of soup to his
mouth, pushed back his plate and rang the bell. Meanwhile,
Neto slowly put down his hat and stick on a chair, charging
the pregnant silence with the slowness of his movements.
Neto was tall and had in his time been handsome. He still had
a good presence, to which his extreme pallor gave a certain air
of refinement and distinction. On his bald head were two
strands of hair, laboriously and quaintly arranged; his greying
moustache seemed to be cleanly clipped with a single scissor
cut, and his slightest movements bore such an affectation of
dignity and earnestness that, even while he was slowly taking
off his gloves, he seemed to be performing an important
formality.

Meanwhile, the maid had brought in the joint, and as she
hovered near the table, dallying in the hope of overhearing a
few words, Neto, with the air of a society man, made a show

of indifference, behaved as usual, saying merely that it had been hot enough to kill.

'Very hot,' echoed Alves, who since Neto's arrival had not raised his eyes from the table edge, leaning back in his chair and fingering his moustache with one hand, the other in his pocket. At last, the maid went out, with orders to wait for a ring on the bell 'to bring in the other things'. Alves got up and went to close the door. Then, seeing that he could speak freely, Neto sat on the edge of his chair, stayed quiet for a moment as he continued to rub his knees. Then he began to speak slowly, his words well chosen and with eloquent intent, seeking to make an impression:

'I quite understood my duty as a father ... '

He paused for a moment, gazing at his son-in-law, waiting for some interruption, just a word. Alves helped himself to rice. Neto went on:

'I understood my duty as a father and I still do so at this moment, which is a solemn one ... As soon as I got the letter, as soon as I saw that there was trouble here in the household, I came to fetch my daughter, to create an interval in which to see whether there might be some explanation, the tangle might be unravelled ... When two people are at loggerheads, it is best for each of them to withdraw to his own side. From a distance, in cold blood, things are more manageable; face to face, word against word, everything gets out of hand ... '

His portentous words were running out; with one banal phrase after another, he spoke excitedly, confusedly:

'And so, what I want to know is, what does all this upset mean?'

Alves had listened to him silently, absentmindedly spearing grains of rice. He was determined not to change his attitude, to remain respectful and aloof. He despised his father-in-law on account of doubtful tales which he knew about him, especially of his disreputable philandering with his cook. That solemn air did not impress him, and with a few laconic words he would easily put him in his place.

'The upset is nothing more nor less than what I wrote and told you. I found your daughter with a man and I ordered her out of the house.'

Neto trembled. That curt tone seemed to him an insult. He stood up, his eyes blazing, his bald head revealing his irritation.

'Well, now! The very idea! And what if I do not want her in my house? That's not bad—you marry a girl of good family, keep her for four years, and then you say "My girl, you are going back to your father!" That's not bad! And what, my dear sir, if I don't want her in my house—if I don't want her in my house?'

He waved his arms, forgetting all his restraint, in a voice that could be heard in the kitchen.

'In that case,' Alves replied very coolly, 'she stays in the street.'

That only infuriated Neto.

'In the street? In the street?'

'Precisely. She dishonoured me, dishonoured my house. I will not tolerate her here ... Let her pack her bags and go! If her father or anyone else will not take her, it is obvious that she stays in the street ... '

Neto could not credit this implacable resolve. He folded his arms and stared at his son-in-law with a burning gaze.

'Let me look at you, man ... Let me look at you, for you are a monster! So you mean to say that you abandon your wife, leave her in the street, with no corner to shelter in?'

Such words tortured Alves. It was like probing a wound that was still bleeding. He got up, wanting to say the word that would put an end to the discussion, but Neto did not let him open his mouth, bawling out:

'And one does not put a wife out of the house just because one finds her alone, receiving a visitor!'

Alves went on looking at him, his lips trembling, unable to utter the words that were choking him. It was an ordeal to utter aloud, in that very place, and even to a father-in-law, how he had found her in another man's embrace. And in face of that silence, Neto grew more confident, triumphant:

'Proofs are necessary! The law requires that one is caught in the act ... You saw nothing, did not find a single letter ... '

Alves's anger erupted:

'Disgraceful letters, sir! Disgusting letters! Do you realise what she said to him, that she would like to have a son by him! A son that I would have to clothe, to feed, to care for, to educate ... A son! And this is the way that you brought up your daughter ... '

Neto was taken aback. His daughter had said nothing to him about the letters. He passed his hand across the two strands on his bald head with an air of distraction; and, after a long silence, he muttered:

'When madness seizes them, women write things without rhyme or reason ... '

Alves did not reply. He paced the room, with his hands in his pockets; on the table, his plate of rice was forgotten, getting cold, drying up. Neto drank a large glass of water and suddenly, like someone coming to a decision, he mentioned the all-important matter that had brought him there:

'But what, after all, do you intend her to live on? I have nothing to clothe her or provide her with shoes ... '

At once, Alves ceased his dejected pacing. He had been waiting for this, he was prepared for it and had his answer ready, introducing into it a touch of dignity, of a man above considerations of money:

'As long as your daughter stays in her father's household and behaves herself, she has thirty milreis a month.'

Neto's bald head fairly glistened and he seemed content, all his anger suddenly disappeared.

'That's reasonable, that is reasonable,' he said in a voice that was almost gentle. And the two men stayed silent, as if there was nothing more to be said. Alves rang the bell, the

The Yellow Sofa 41

servant came at once, darting an inquisitive glance from one to the other as she came in.

'The coffee,' said Alves.

'And bring a cup for me, Senhora Margarida,' added Neto, quickly resuming the homely familiarity of a father-in-law.

Alves went on pacing about the room. Neto sat down at the table and was carefully rolling a cigarette, glancing now and then at his son-in-law. He took an age to make the cigarette, rolling it slowly, full and smooth, and putting the tobacco pouch in his pocket, he exclaimed, with a little sigh:

'The worst thing is the tittle-tattle!'

Alves said nothing; the other struck a match and lit his cigarette with deliberation.

'And with your position in business, it can do you nothing but harm . . .'

Alves turned on him impatiently:

'And whose fault is that?'

That was the point, the fault was not his, Neto knew that very well. But, after all, it would be better to avoid gossip, at least in these early days.

Margarida came in with the coffee. Alves had sat down. As they stirred the sugar, father-in-law and son-in-law face to face were silent for a moment. Neto tried his coffee, added more sugar. Then he took a couple of puffs and returned to his theme:

'Neither for you, nor for me, is it a good thing that they should start talking in the neighbourhood...'

His slowness, these pauses, irritated Alves:

'So what the deuce do you want me to do?'

Still Neto maintained his calm reflective air. And in a low voice, he spoke about his feelings. He had always considered himself a good father; and if his circumstances had been different, he would not have accepted the monthly allowance for his daughter... he would have asked for nothing. He would have taken her home; they would all have lived there together, and that would have been that... and he for his part would have done everything possible to put an end to the scandal.

Alves began to understand. Neto had a plan for getting more money out of him. He wanted to have matters cleared up quickly:

'Come on, let me know what you have in mind, without any more beating about the bush.'

Still Neto was evasive. The best way of avoiding scandal was to go away from Lisbon... and the season was in their favour, it was the time for going to the seaside... No one would be surprised if he were to go away, for example, to Ericeira, taking his married daughter with him. Everyone would assume that Alves, because of his business, was unable to accompany her... But no one would know whether or not he went to visit his wife each Sunday. It was a fine idea, but... Alves broke in:

'And you want me to give you the money for it...'

'But not if I am going to rob you,' confessed the other, with great frankness.

Alves reflected. That would be a clever way of going to spend the summer at the seaside at his expense; but at the same time, the idea was practical, would kill the gossip ... He accepted. And in a moment they settled the details. Alves would contribute towards the cost of a house, to the travelling, to moving certain items of furniture; during the months of August, September and October, the allowance to Neto's daughter would be increased to fifty milreis, to cover expenses at the seaside. Having said all this, he got up, wanting by any means to bring the interview to a close.

'Let us not discuss things any further, for my head is swimming.'

Indeed, he was as pale as a corpse, with a headache coming on, a desire to lie down, go to sleep and forget for a long time.

Yet Neto, on his feet, still wanted to say one last word. From now on, he would be the person responsible for his daughter. He had faith in God, he felt certain that, later on, when the first shock had passed, there would be a better understanding between the couple and they would come together again.

With a sad smile, Alves shook his head in disagreement; no, he would never again be reconciled with her.

'The future belongs to God,' said Neto. 'At the moment, I agree that it is better that you should be separated for a while.

And I should like to end with this: while she is in my house, it will be as though she were in a convent. I am answerable for her.'

Alves shrugged his shoulders a little. All this seemed to him idle chatter. What he now wanted was to be alone. He had rung for Margarida so that she could open the door and show Senhor Neto out. The latter took up his hat and, already on his feet, drank the last gulp of coffee and, after shaking hands with his son-in-law, went out, quietly telling the maid to have the mistress's luggage ready.

'And she told me to say that you were not to forget the silver sugar caster that her godfather gave her on her birthday, the sugar caster is hers ...'

And he went down the stairs, congratulating himself on that bright idea. His daughter had not even mentioned the sugar caster. But, after all, it was hers, a nice piece of silver, it was right that it too should go back home.

Outdoors, the evening was sultry and Neto slowly made his way home, hat in hand, well pleased with himself, working out the expenses for the stay in Ericeira. The seaside holiday was going to do him good. With Ludovina's fifty milreis a month, one could be comfortable, and since she ought not to be appearing in public, there would be no expensive outfits, so he would be putting money in his pocket!

When he had climbed his hundred and fifty steps, a few at a time, he rang the doorbell and it was his unmarried daughter,

Teresa, who came to let him in, her eyes shining, quite excited. No one had hidden the truth from her. She already knew that Ludovina had been caught with a man, that there had been a big row, and that her father had gone to have it out with Alves.

'Well?' she asked anxiously.

'Indoors, we will talk indoors,' said Neto.

They went through the kitchen which was in semi-darkness, lit only by the brightness of the coal fire in the stove, on which the kettle was boiling, and they came to the dining-room, a sort of cubbyhole at the rear of the flat. Sitting at a round table covered with oilcloth, the maid, Joanna, a lively young woman wearing the expensive earrings of a lady and dressed in a blue merino cloth, was reading the daily newspaper by the light of an oil lamp. In the shadow, next to the sideboard, was Ludovina, stretched out in a wicker chair.

When her father appeared, she got up, dressed all in black, her eyes still red. Neto sat down, wiping his neck with a silk handkerchief. The eyes of the three women devoured him, and as he was in no hurry, enjoying the family's suspense, it was Joanna who cried out to him:

'Come on then, out with it!'

He slowly folded up the handkerchief and, in the pregnant silence of the room, replied:

'Godofredo is giving thirty milreis a month.'

They breathed a low sigh of relief, there was a stir of

satisfaction. Teresa looked at her sister, astonished at those thirty milreis, coming into anyone's purse like that, just through being caught with a man! Joanna admitted that he was a gentleman. But Ludovina saw nothing extraordinary in it; it was *he* who had been at fault, who had put her out of the house without a bean! Then her father turned to her, his brow puckered:

'After all, you say you had written nothing, but he says he caught you with improper letters.'

'It's a lie,' she said simply, 'the letters meant nothing, it was just a joke.'

There was silence. Gazing at the table edge, Neto was arranging the hair strands of his bald pate, in a dignified way. And the three women went on staring at him, awaiting more details, the full story of the interview.

'And Lulu's luggage, Papa?' asked Teresa who, since the previous evening, had been living in hopes of watching the suitcases arrive, seeing them unpacked, picking up a present. But Papa, following his own line of thought, without answering the girl, went on:

'And in order to avoid gossip, it was agreed that we should go and spend the summer at Ericeira.'

Then there was a joyful outburst. Teresa clapped her hands, Joanna smiled with satisfaction, for she so much wanted to go to the seaside. Only Ludovina remained indifferent, her face clouded with sadness, thinking about the fine plans that Godofredo had recently been discussing –

the months of August and September to be spent in Sintra...
And she went and sat down again, while Joanna and Teresa,
already full of plans, plied Neto with questions, both full of
enthusiasm for that unexpected seaside holiday. And already
there were a thousand projects. Teresa chattered endlessly,
Joanna mentioned the things that they would need to take –
mattresses, crockery, and the piano, for greater enjoyment. It
would be best for all of them to go to Ericeira and find a
house. Then Ludovina broke her silence:

'And a house is needed in which there is sufficient space.
For I am not disposed to sleep in a cubicle, like the one here.'

In face of this demand, Papa shook his head. And he did
not mince words, but said at once:

'You've got to sleep where you can... If you wanted the
comforts of your husband's house, you should have behaved
yourself and stayed there.'

There was an embarrassed silence. No one dared to answer
back when Neto raised his voice. So in the respectful silence
evoked by his annoyed tone, he drew closer to the table, took
a pencil from his pocket, set his spectacles on his nose, and
under the oil lamp, began to work out, on the white margin
of the newspaper, his estimate of the expenses for Ericeira.

Stretching across the table, Teresa saw those figures lining
up – so much for the house, so much for a carriage to take
them there – like a string of pleasures, shining out from the
figures. Standing opposite to her, Joanna was giving her
opinion. In the kitchen, the kettle went on boiling...

48 *The Yellow Sofa*

Virtuous tranquillity enveloped the house – and in the shadow, Ludovina was silent, as though crushed by the existence which now awaited her; the discomforts, poor food, her father's temperament, the maid's position of authority in the house – everything that lay in store for her and everything that she had lost. She cursed her own stupidity for falling like that into the arms of a man she did not love, from whom she derived no pleasure, brought to her present pass for no real reason, through a mere whim and through having nothing to do.

5 ⚡ NEXT MORNING, A SHAFT OF SUNLIGHT SHINING through the window awoke Alves abruptly. He quickly sat up, leaning on his elbow, and as he rubbed his eyes, he was astounded to find himself on the sofa, fully dressed and wearing his shoes. Then, like a blow, the recall of his trouble fell heavily on his heart. A dark veil seemed to cover everything around him.

The previous night, after Neto had gone, he had stretched out there, dead tired, and had quickly fallen into a deep and heavy sleep.

He sat up on the sofa. In the house and in the street profound silence reigned: it was only six o'clock. Around him, the room still showed the disorder of the previous day, with the suitcases in the centre, the negligee at the foot of the double bed. He gazed at the bed in which no one had slept, with the two pillows side by side. Then, as on the previous evening, he paced around; in the dining-room, the table still bore the previous day's tablecloth, and on the sideboard a forgotten candle had guttered and gone out in the candlestick.

As he faced the drawing-room, cowardice seized him; he did not dare to draw the curtains. And he returned to the bedroom, sat down again, his hands purposeless, his gaze vacant, not knowing what he ought to do at that early hour when the city was still sleeping. At that hour, Ludovina certainly would also be asleep.

And he remembered mornings when, while he was still asleep, she would wake early, get up quietly and open a fanlight in the window, her beautiful tresses in a hair-net, the lace of her nightdress covering her breast and her long dark eyelashes shading her face . . . . Now, in that bright early morning light, the undisturbed bed gave him a painful feeling of coldness and discomfort. Despondency gripped him, an immense and unending wretchedness ate into his spirit, made him want to lay his head on the arm of the sofa and sit there until he died. And, as on the previous day, the thought of death returned, penetrating his spirit with the gentle softness of a caress . . .

Within a few hours, everything would be resolved— perhaps he would be dead. It was at ten o'clock that he was to meet the other man. His heart pounded at the thought of seeing him again, face to face, and it seemed impossible to visualise him in any posture other than the one in which he had seen him the previous day, with his arm round her waist. And his idea of the previous evening—suicide decided by drawing lots—which had seemed so natural, now made him afraid. It seemed odd that he, Alves, there in that house in São Bento Street, with the morning sun lighting it up, should have had that grim idea, more appropriate to a violent character. So he was greatly worried. What would the other one say to such a proposition? What if he were to refuse? And other difficulties of detail would arise. How would they draw lots—with blank slips of paper? And he grew fearful that, faced with so preposterous a suggestion, the other man would merely laugh .... In which case, he would box his ears! But no, he could not refuse, he was a man of honour. At all events, he would know very soon. And he did not want to think about that; the idea kept him going, almost saved him from suffering and even gave him some sort of self-respect, lessening the sense of ridicule. He did not want to dwell on anything that might lessen the importance of his plan.

Meanwhile, he heard footsteps in the kitchen: the maids had got up. In the street, noise was growing, the voices of street-criers, passing carts, the confused hum of a city coming to life. And then, little by little, he began to follow his daily routine, put the cuff links into his clean shirt, sharpen his razor ... But the big trunk in the middle of the room got in his way.

Suddenly, it occurred to him that he ought to make his will. Before the mirror, motionless, with his face half lathered, he went on turning it over in his mind – and a sort of dread amazement took hold of him, at being there in his own bedroom, in his shirt-sleeves, calmly thinking about dying. For all those ideas which in the excitement of the evening had seemed so natural and easy were assuming in the clear light of morning, in the routine of his toilet, a false, unnatural, aspect which was at odds with his real personality.

At eight o'clock, the doorbell rang. He went and listened; on the landing, women's voices were speaking. Then a maid came in and went out – he asked who it was. It was Neto's maid. But he did not venture to ask more questions, or what it was she wanted.

Then there was breakfast. He ate ravenously. He wondered why the ham was not on the table and the maid, when she brought it, told him that the mistress would be sending for the cases in the evening. He said nothing. Increasingly, he detested Margarida, who seemed to be continuing to watch over her mistress's interests, getting messages from her, still her confidante. And as the sugar caster was missing, Alves was annoyed, made much of its absence, threatened to throw her out. As the girl was in the corridor, muttering, he shouted angrily:

'Less noise.'

All the time his chest was tightening at the thought of meeting the other man. Fearful of crossing the street, where his misfortune was perhaps already being talked about, he ordered a cab. The maid dawdled. Time was passing, and nervously, almost in a fever, he moved between the window and the front door, putting on his gloves, and feeling that the floor on which he was walking was insubstantial, giving way beneath his feet. At last, the cab arrived and he went down, his throat constricted in awful agitation. His voice nearly dried up as he gave the cab driver the address. Once on its way, the cab seemed to fly, and in his excited state his stomach kept turning over, his breakfast heaved in his throat. At last it got there. And he was so confused that he could not find in his pocket the right coin to pay the driver.

The office was asleep in the profound holiday silence, and when he pushed open the green baize door, the clock was striking ten, in the hollow tone to which the low ceiling gave that doleful, mourning resonance. He went quickly to his room; it seemed as though he had not been there for an age, and that there was something different about the furniture and the arrangement of things. The bunch of flowers had completely withered in its vase.

His mood suddenly changed. Facing that furniture, those two partners' desks, one alongside the other, reminding him of the intimacy, the mutual confidence, of the years, the very furniture shared his anger and he was seized with a dreadful rage. Well, Machado was a villain who deserved to die! And every object, even the walls, as though saturated with the business integrity which belonged there, were a silent accusation against his partner's treachery. Suddenly, a light footstep sounded outside: it was Machado.

The Yellow Sofa 53

Instinctively, Alves took refuge behind his desk, sorting papers at random with trembling hands and without daring to lift his eyes.

The door opened and Machado entered, white as a corpse, with his hat and stick in one hand, the other in his trouser pocket, revealing a bulge. But Alves did not notice it, did not dare look at it, his glance roamed here and there, searching for a word, something profound and dignified to say. At last, with an effort, he faced him and at once that hand in the pocket gave him a fright; he started involuntarily, fearing a weapon, an attack. Machado understood, slowly took his hand out of his pocket and went to put his hat and stick on his desk. Then Alves, trembling, in anxious haste to break the silence, stammered:

'After what happened yesterday, we cannot go on being friends.'

Machado, whose drawn face wore an anxious expression, closed his eyes, breathed more freely. He too had been expecting an act of violence, something dreadful; and the moderation, the sad groan of a friendship betrayed, surprised him, deeply impressed him. At that moment, he would have liked to throw himself into his partner's arms. And it was with genuine emotion, a sob in his throat, that he replied:

'Unhappily, unhappily…'

Alves then beckoned to him to sit down. Machado, crestfallen, went and sat on the edge of the repp sofa. Alves let himself fall like an inert mass on to the stool by the desk.

And for a while, complete silence reigned, made even deeper by that city street in its Sunday quiet. Alves passed a trembling hand across his face, searching for words. The other waited, staring at the carpet.

'A duel between us is impossible,' said Alves at last, with an effort.

'I am at your service, the decision is yours...'

'It is impossible,' said Alves again. 'We'd be laughed at... Especially the sort of duels that go on around here... It would make us ridiculous... We cannot do it in our position... All business men would laugh at a duel between partners...'

For a moment, Alves was silent, working on the thought that they were partners and on the past which had bound them together. He had not felt Machado's infamy so sharply until he saw him there, in that office room, where they had worked together for three years. And he exclaimed:

'There is no word to describe your infamous behaviour...'

He had risen, his voice grew louder, and his feeling of a friend betrayed gave his words dignity, a solemnity which crushed the other man. He spoke quietly, aiming his words at him, like blows. He had known him from childhood, had looked after him in his young days; he had made him his partner, his friend, opened his home to him, welcomed him like a brother!

'And behind my back, what do you do? Dishonour me!'

The Yellow Sofa 55

Machado stood up, with a distressed look, wanting to be done with the torture.

'I know all that,' he stammered, 'and I am ready to make amends in full, whatever they may be.'

Excitedly, Alves then revealed his plan:

'The only reparation is this: one of us must die ... A duel is absurd ... Let us draw lots for which of us must kill himself.'

As soon as he had uttered them, those pathetic words seemed like strange and disconnected sounds; the quiet atmosphere, the very office furniture seemed to spurn them. Yet he had said the words, and he felt relieved at having finally got off his mind the idea which, since the previous evening, had been filling him with anxiety and torment.

Machado went on looking at him, his eyes staring.

'Draw lots? In what way draw lots?'

He seemed not to understand. The suicide drawn by lots seemed to him grotesque and insane. And as Alves stayed by his desk, saying nothing but nervously twirling his moustache, Machado grew impatient and exclaimed:

'Are you serious? Do you really mean it?'

Then it was Alves who looked at him, downcast. What he feared had come to pass. Machado had found it absurd and had refused. His anger grew as he saw vengeance eluding him.

'Even yesterday you ran away, fled in a cowardly manner when I caught you. Now you want to run away from this as well!'

Livid, the other man shouted:

'Run away from what?'

Silent rage possessed him, made his eyes blaze. The other's accusations had exasperated him. Then there had come this absurd suggestion, of a suicide drawn by lot. Now he was insulting him! No, he could not put up with that! And excited now, he stammered:

'Run away from what?' he repeated, 'Run away from what? I am not running away from anything...'

'In that case,' said Alves, banging his fist on the desk, 'let us draw lots, here and now, to decide which of us must disappear!'

For a moment, Machado looked at him with cold disdain, as though he might strangle him. Then he quickly snatched up his hat and stick, and at the door, in a biting, emphatic and vibrant voice, said:

'I am ready to give you full satisfaction, even with my life... But it must be in a sane and proper way, with four witnesses, with swords or pistols as you prefer, at whatever distance you choose, a mortal duel, whatever your wish. I am at your disposal. All today, all tomorrow, I shall be waiting at home. But I do not understand the ideas of a madman. And we have nothing more to discuss!'

So Alves remained there, alone with the lamentable ruins of his grand design, humiliated, confused, annoyed, his temples throbbing, and not knowing what he ought to do!

6 🪶 IN THE END, HE GRABBED HIS HAT, JUST AS Machado had done, and left the office. And he was so shattered that he was already in Gold Street when he realised that he had not locked up; he went back and that seemed to restore some sense of order to his thoughts.

He had decided to fight him, in a duel to the death, and nothing on earth seemed capable of satisfying him except to see Machado at his feet, with a bullet in his heart.

So what? That fellow had dishonoured him, robbed him of his wife's affection and now, on top of everything, had treated him like an imbecile, called him mad! That especially infuriated him, because he now felt uneasily that there was in fact something ridiculous in the idea of suicide drawn by lot. Perhaps so! But Machado should not have said so, ought to have accepted everything, resigned himself to the form of reparation that he had demanded. Had he not asked only for natural and reasonable amends? Very well, so be it; they would fight with pistols – but only one of them loaded, taken at random and aimed from the distance of a handkerchief's width. Then there would still be an element of chance, of fate, leaving everything in the just hands of God!

Meanwhile, he would go at once to Rossio, where his close friend, Carvalho, lived – he who had been Director of Customs at Cape Verde and had married well. He headed in that direction, for he was the first person to whom he would want to go, and he would tell him everything, relying on his old friendship. Then they would go and seek another of his intimate friends, Teles Medeiros, a man of fortune and social standing who had whole armouries of rapiers in his lounge and much experience on any point of honour.

It was nearing mid-day; the July sun was burning up the streets; and the closed shops, people in their Sunday clothes, carriages in the Square drawn up on the shady side, all intensified the feeling of peace and inactivity. A fine haze obscured the blue sky and the sound of bells fell heavily on the gentle air. As Alves was going up Carvalho's steps, he met him coming down, self-important and cool in his new light tweed suit, putting on his pearl-grey gloves. Alves's breathless appearance, his worried air, alarmed Carvalho; and he turned to go up again, opened the door with his key, took him into a little study which contained a bookcase and a wicker chaise-longue, shaped like a camp-bed. In the adjoining room, the lounge, someone was playing the piano, a brisk waltz, making the very house shake.

Carvalho drew the door curtain, closed the window, and only then did he ask 'What is it?'

Alves put his hat on the corner of the table and with a rush straightway unburdened himself. At the opening words—sofa, arm round waist—Carvalho, who was slowly taking off his gloves, stood petrified in the centre of the study; and he went to draw the curtain still more closely, as if he feared that the account of the betrayal might spread an obscene breath over his respectable establishment. Still, in the confused way in which Alves recounted his fate, the impatience with which Carvalho listened, he did not realise who the man had been; he merely assumed that Machado had been present, and when he realised that Machado himself had been the man on the sofa, he slapped one hand against the other and exclaimed in horror:

'What infamy!'

'A man who was like a brother to me,' said Alves, lowering his voice, brandishing his fists, 'and that's how he repays me! No, he must die! I demand a duel to the death . . .'

Carvalho's full-bearded face then showed a disturbed expression. Now he understood: Alves had not come merely to unburden himself; he had come to get a second! And at once the timidity of the bureaucrat took hold of him: respect for the law, dread of compromising himself. His self-esteem was revolted in face of the violent and disturbing matters which confronted him. He quickly sought excuses, explanations. If in fact Alves had seen nothing more than – if it was just a matter of their being together in the drawing-room – it might have been a prank, a trifle . . .

Alves searched feverishly through his pockets. The piano in the adjoining room launched now into a jumble of uncertain notes, as if fingers were groping, seeking a forgotten melody. Suddenly, a snatch from *Rigoletto* broke out jerkily, wailing and sobbing. And Alves, who had at last found what he was seeking, put the letter before Carvalho who read it out in a subdued voice: 'My soul's darling, what an afternoon that was yesterday...'

As though the words, heard in someone else's voice, seemed even more disgraceful than when he had read them himself, Alves could not contain himself but raised his voice and shouted:

'No! Only with bloodshed; it must be a duel to the death!'

Carvalho was worried, motioned to him to be quiet. And as the piano had stopped for a moment, he went on listening, fearing that the shouts might have been overheard.

'It is Mariana,' he said, pointing towards the drawing-room. 'For the moment, it is better that she does not know.'

Then, once more, he slowly read the letter, felt the paper, examined it again, holding it in his fingers with excited curiosity, as if he could feel in it the very heat of those kisses... And Alves once more searched through his pockets, annoyed at having forgotten the other letters; for there were others even worse! Gripped now by the wish really to convince Carvalho that his wife was an immoral woman, he quoted phrases, revealed the whole episode, all Ludovina's shamelessness.

'What is more, she did not deny it, she admitted it all!'

'What! You actually spoke to each other?'

After a pause, Alves then completed his confidences, his idea of suicide by lots, his encounter with Machado. Carvalho, who had flung himself on the chaise-longue as though he were shattered, crushed, by all these revelations, opened wide the eyes in that sunburnt face of his, tanned by the Cape Verde sun, shocked that such violent and terrible things had really happened and been recounted to him, there in his quiet Rossio home.

When Alves related how Machado had considered the whole idea senseless, Carvalho did not restrain himself:

'Madness indeed! Pure madness!' he exclaimed, as he got up.

And in the narrow study, waving his arms about, he sought a word, a phrase, to sum it all up, went on talking of 'madness' and ended by saying that such things happened only in *Rocambole*!

'It comes to the same thing,' said Alves. 'For I insist that it must be a pistol duel, but with only one of them loaded, and that drawn by lot ... '

Carvalho gave a start: 'Only one pistol, drawn by lot? But that is murder! No, please do not count on me! There is no justification for that ... And even if there were, I would not meddle in such a matter.'

Perceiving himself deserted, Alves was indignant. So, in this desperate crisis, he, his best friend, was going to leave him in the lurch like that? On whom, then, ought he to rely, to whom trust his honour?

The other man rambled on, again spoke of assassination, of crime, of prison, and ended by saying:

'If you were to come and ask me to set fire to the Bank of Portugal, do you think that I ought to agree?'

Alves tried to explain that it was not the same thing; their voices grew louder, one against the other, when a pause in the piano playing made them break off. There was an argument in the adjoining room, voices were raised, an altercation in which could be heard the words 'white skirt', 'slattern', 'Madam said nothing', all uttered in a tone of annoyance. For a moment, Carvalho listened. Then he shrugged his shoulders: it must be some new neglect on the part of the maid, a shameless creature whom they had had for a month, and who did nothing properly. Then, hearing a door slammed, he could not resist going to see what was the matter.

Left alone for a moment, Alves felt a great weariness taking hold of him. Since the previous day his nerves had been on edge, taut as the strings of a tightly tuned violin. Until now, everything had seemed to him so easy, his vengeance secure. But now he had had two shocks in quick succession. Machado had not been in favour of suicide by lot; and now this fellow did not want any duel to the death! And something within him began to weaken, as if his spirit was growing weary of maintaining, for so many hours, a sombre attitude of vengeance and death. His head began to ache, the headache that had been threatening him since the previous evening. He sat down on the chaise-longue, his head in his hands, and sighed profoundly.

Carvalho returned, flushed and excited. There had been a scene, he had thrown the servant girl out. Then he became upset, complained of his bad luck that did not allow him an honest maidservant – all a mob of shameless hussies, slatterns who cheated him. He remembered nostalgically the coloured ones – there was nothing to compare with a coloured maid.

'So tell me what you think about all this affair,' asked Alves, in disillusionment.

Carvalho shrugged his shoulders:

'The best thing is to leave everything as it is, your wife in her father's home, you in yours, and what will be will be . . . '

Yet he felt a touch of remorse, wanted to show sympathy, and added:

'In this whole affair, count on me entirely . . . A proper duel, with swords, or even with pistols, to preserve your honour, yes sir! I'm on! But not those tragic affairs! No!'

Taking up his hat, Alves said:

'Let us go and see what Medeiros has to say; let's go to Teles Medeiros's house!'

Carvalho was crestfallen. He was going to spend the day with his wife, at the home of her parents at Pedrouças. It was his brother-in-law's birthday . . . But, after all, in such an affair, it was necessary to do something for one's friends.

'Let us go, then, just let me tell Mariana that I can't go with her . . . '

When, shortly afterwards, he came back, putting on his gloves, he looked irritable and disagreeable. On the way downstairs he stopped and turned to Alves, who was following him down:

'Did you know that my wife is expecting, eh?...A shock could be fatal, and if she were to know that I was a second...It's no joke...However, let us go. Friends are for such occasions...'

Down below, they took a carriage, for Medeiros lived down town, near the Estrela. It was a two-seater, almost new, smart and shining, which rolled noiselessly along. This put Carvalho into a better humour and he leaned back, finished buttoning his gloves. For a while, they did not exchange a word. Then, when the coupé was going through Loreto, a great curiosity seemed to take hold of Carvalho. Alves had given him few details. What had Ludovina said? How had he got to know of the affair? What had Neto said? Alves, seeming weary and downcast, completed the story in a few brief words. His friend did not approve of the thirty milreis allowance: it was 'an indulgence to disgraceful behaviour'. But seeing that Alves looked dejected, that he was biting his lip with emotion, and his eyes filled with tears, Carvalho murmured vaguely:

'This life is just a mess!'

They did not exchange another word until they reached Medeiros's house. When they rang the bell, the maid told them that Senhor Medeiros was still in bed. So Carvalho went upstairs, went familiarly into Medeiros's bedroom, making a noise, calling him a lazy-bones and a roué. Behind him, Alves was knocking into the furniture, in the gloom of the bedroom.

From the shade of the bed curtains, Medeiros's ill-humoured voice demanded to know what sort of invasion this was; and when they opened the curtains, he cried out, buried himself in the sheets, unable to bear the bright morning light. But at last he showed his sleep-drenched face; then he roused himself, raised himself on to his elbow, and took a cigarette from the bedside table.

Carvalho sat down beside the bed, and for a while they chatted about the idle ways of Medeiros, who explained that he had got to bed at five that morning.

Then Carvalho began:

'We have come here about a very serious matter...'

His friend interrupted him, calling out for the manservant. He wanted to know whether a letter had arrived that morning. The youth brought it in his pocket. Sitting up in bed, with his hair dishevelled, Medeiros opened it nervously, glanced quickly over it and, with a sigh of relief, put it under his pillow.

'My goodness, I was almost caught out yesterday. A matter of a moment... And if her husband had come into the kitchen, which is immediately next to the door, he would have discovered just how faithful his Maria is. Well, didn't I have a shock!'

Carvalho and Alves exchanged glances, and Carvalho uttered this pregnant phrase:

'Well, it's about something of that kind that we have come here...'

And he went on:

'Alves has had an unfortunate experience.'

And under Medeiros's staring gaze, Alves suddenly found himself choked by the feeling of his ridiculousness. He saw himself as belonging to the grotesque tribe of betrayed husbands who cannot come home without some lover making his escape... And it was like that throughout the city, scandal in corners, lovers fleeing and lovers caught... He had caught one of them. This fellow Medeiros would have been caught out if the husband had come into the kitchen – and he seemed to see throughout the city a sarabande of lovers and husbands, some of them escaping, husbands pursuing them, a hide-and-seek of men chasing each other around women's skirts! And again he felt the weariness, dread of having yet again to tell his lamentable tale.

But Medeiros's eyes, his face, were expectant, questioning, so with a peculiar expression he said at last:

'It was yesterday. I caught Ludovina with Machado.'

'By Jove!' exclaimed Medeiros, starting up in the bed.

And putting out his cigarette, quickly taking another, he wanted to know the details. But it was Carvalho, now the spokesman, who gave them, relishing his part, giving details of the affair, with all the confidence of the husband of a rich nincompoop, whom no one had ever tempted... He told it all, while Alves, slumped in an armchair, with his top hat still in his hand, went on nodding his head in confirmation.

In the end, Medeiros said: 'Let me see the letter.'

So Alves once more took it from his wallet, and yet again heard a stranger's voice murmur those words of his wife's: 'Darling of my soul, what an afternoon that was . . .'

Medeiros, in his nightshirt, recalling Ludovina's dark eyes, her heavenly body, excitedly repeated the phrase, fingering the paper, with all his senses visualising what had happened. And he too was immediately seized with a terrible rage against Machado. Deuce take it, he must indeed be a vile wretch! In fact, he already had some faults on record . . . deuce take it, when the ladies wanted something, one could not be a Joseph of Egypt . . . but never with the wife of an intimate friend, let alone of a colleague . . .

'That calls for blood,' he said excitedly, jumping into the middle of the bedroom in his nightshirt and his slippered feet.

At once, salvaging his courage, Alves exclaimed:

'I was wanting a duel to the death, but this chap says no...'

Carvalho then appealed to his friend Medeiros. Was the idea of a single loaded pistol, chosen at random, by any chance reasonable?

Medeiros looked at them in astonishment. No! Certainly not! There was no justification for that, nor . . .

It was the second time that Alves had heard there was no justification. And he burst out, excitedly:

'So there is no justification? No justification! So what sort of justification would be sufficient for two men to kill each other?'

'Spitting in one's face or some such thing,' said Medeiros authoritatively, still in his nightshirt, as he began rapidly to comb his hair.

Alves wanted to argue, but the other, turning round with the comb in his hand, put an end to his questioning.

'Even if there had been justification, I would not take on a thing like that. I do not meddle in such matters.'

'There you have it!' exclaimed Carvalho, in triumph. 'What did I tell you? No one wants such a responsibility. More especially myself, with a wife who is expecting . . . I say, what a mess . . .'

Alves was downcast. And yet, in his innermost heart, he began to feel relieved, as though some of the indecision which he had had since the previous evening had vanished and something definite had emerged. Now it had been settled that there would be no lots or chances, that there was not to be the death of a man; and in the confused state in which he had been until then, this made a fixed point, a basis, a decision on which he could rely. Nor was it he who had so decided, it was his closest friends, who had reasoned it out in cold blood . . . But, anyhow, leaving aside the death of one of them, something still had to be done.

'So what do you two advise? What is to be done? I cannot stay like this, with my arms folded . . .'

Medeiros, standing in the middle of the room, in his shirt, showing his thin legs with his feet in his big slippers, solemnly exclaimed:

'Do you wish to place your honour in my hands, in our hands?'

Obviously, he was willing; he was there for no other purpose.

'Very well,' said Medeiros, 'then you have nothing more to worry about. Let yourself be guided: we shall arrange everything.'

And he withdrew into a little cubicle, where they heard him cleaning his teeth, rinsing his mouth, making a great noise in the wash basin.

Still Alves seemed unsatisfied; he went to the door of the cubicle, wanting to know...

'There's nothing you can know,' shouted the other from within, noisily washing himself with sponge and water. 'Nor can we know... We have first to go to Machado, see what he has to say, consult with his seconds, and so on... Go home and don't go out until we come. And leave us the cab, do you hear, to make all these journeyings... On Sundays, one brushes one's black morning coat, with black shoes, everything in black...'

Hearing this, Carvalho glanced at his own light tweed suit. But he did not agree with these sartorial niceties; with a clean shirt on his back, a man was fit to go anywhere.

Meanwhile, Alves was pacing the room, deep in thought. And at last he told Carvalho what was worrying him:

'It is essential that you lay down firm conditions. And apart from using pistols at twenty paces, I...'

'Leave all that to Medeiros,' Carvalho broke in.

Medeiros, coming in at that moment, with the towel in his hand, his hair dry, went on:

'Look here, you know about business affairs. But I understand about affairs of honour. From now on, you have only to wait until we come and tell you – it is at such a time, in such a place, with such and such weapons. And then, on the following day, off you go! You don't even have to worry yourself about a doctor. I shall ask Gomes, who knows a lot about wounds... He is not a man to panic if one of you is badly wounded.'

Alves felt a shudder go down his spine and his chest tighten. But from one side, Carvalho was saying to him:

'So go home, if you have anything to do, papers to put in order, or anything else...'

He did not mention a will but the allusion was so clear that it annoyed the worthy Alves.

Certainly, he had at first wanted the duel to be serious, even to the death, but after all, those two – his best friends, his cronies, one of them already talking about wounds and the other pushing him out of the door so that he might go and make his will – it seemed to him tactless and needlessly cruel. Without a word, he went downstairs and left. And flinging himself into the back of the coupé, his spirits dampened and his body wet, he had this profound reflection:

'And it is for this that people marry, for this that one wishes to have a family!...'

7 ✠ THAT EVENING AT SIX O'CLOCK, ALVES WAS IN his slippers, having just finished sealing up a bundle of papers in his study, when the bell rang and his two friends appeared.

Despite his indifference to convention, Carvalho had gone and changed his suit, was wearing a black frock-coat, and they both looked very solemn. Medeiros, now very correct with his waxed moustache, sat down on the sofa and began slowly to take off his black gloves as he peered at Alves. Then he said:

'So you are bursting with curiosity? Well, look here, nothing has yet been settled.'

Very pale and with staring eyes, Alves seemed to breathe more easily. But he suddenly flared up: why had nothing been settled? So had the scoundrel refused him reparation?

'No!' Carvalho retorted. 'To everyone his due; in this matter, Machado is behaving well.'

'So?'

'It was the seconds who had reservations,' said Medeiros. 'This is what happened.'

It was a long story that Medeiros told, long-windedly, relishing the details. They had spoken to Machado, who had promised that two of his friends would be at his, Medeiros's, house at four o'clock. And punctually, Nunes Vidal, whom Alves knew well, had turned up there – a young man of experience in affairs of honour – accompanied by Cunha,

Albert Cunha, who had little to say, was there only to make up the number. They came in, there were the usual greetings, etcetera … all very serious but everything very friendly. Then they came to the question. Nunes Vidal began by affirming that Senhor Machado was in principle ready to accept all the conditions proposed by Senhor Alves – all of them, whatever they might be, in their entirety. But he, Nunes Vidal, and his friend Cunha understood it to be the duty of the seconds in a dispute first of all to seek peace and reconciliation. If, however, their principal, Senhor Machado, through an excess of self-esteem and pride, was in principle disposed to allow himself to be killed, his seconds, who had taken his interests into their keeping, were there, and had come there not merely to seek, as far as possible, to avoid disaster happening to their friend in the field, but also to avoid any scandal which might be prejudicial to his name.

'All this was very well stated,' Medeiros added, 'all very well explained, in well-chosen words … Frankly, I liked Vidal.'

'Ah! a young man of great talent,' murmured Carvalho.

Finally, Vidal had wound up by saying that, all things considered, he did not think there was any justification for a serious duel with pistols.

Again that absence of justification! Alves demurred:

'A thousand devils! Then what more damage would this ass have wanted Machado to do to me?'

With a gesture, Medeiros restrained himself:

'Don't excite yourself, man, don't get worked up ... Let it suffice that I have told you everything. Vidal is most experienced, but, mind you, I did not take it in silence. Ask Carvalho ... '

'He behaved like a hero,' said Carvalho.

'But what the devil did Vidal say after that?' Alves insisted.

Vidal had said that there was no excuse for bloodshed, because what had happened between Machado and the lady had been a mere flirtation ...

Alves made a furious gesture. And Medeiros, also getting to his feet, said:

'Don't get excited, man! Listen! Then I told him the whole story. I told him how you had caught them, and the letters, "My darling, what an afternoon yesterday", and the rest. I put before him all the facts in order to convince him that adultery had been complete ... Isn't that the truth, Carvalho?'

'Absolutely!'

'I told him plainly: my principal, our friend Alves, is in every sense of the word a husband who ... in short, he wants amends. Isn't that the truth, Carvalho?'

Carvalho made a gesture of agreement.

'But Vidal proved the contrary to me; he, too, read the letters, Machado told him everything; and after conferring, thinking it over, they arrived at the conclusion that it had not gone beyond a flirtation.'

In the room, silence reigned. Alves paced about hurriedly, his hands in his pockets. Carvalho looked absently at a picture representing Leda and the Swan. Suddenly, Alves stopped, and speaking slowly in a muffled voice, said:

'There, on that sofa, I saw them with their arms around each other. What does Vidal say to that?'

'That is the crucial point,' exclaimed Medeiros. 'It is a fact that cannot be denied, because you saw it with your very eyes. But Machados gave an explanation to Nunes and Nunes explained it to us. It was a joke, it was in fun, he did it to tickle her!'

'And the letter: "What an afternoon yesterday"?', Alves exclaimed.

'Nunes said that it refers, of course, to a walk you took to Belem . . . You did go to Belem?'

Alves thought for a moment. Yes, they had been to Belem . . . It was quite true that all three of them had gone together to Belem.

'Then there you are. It was to recall the pleasure of having gone, all three of you, for an outing, for a stroll . . .'

'So that was all there was in it?' said Alves. 'It was nothing; I have to put up with the insult!'

Medeiros, indignant, stood up. Well now, so what did he take him for? Had Alves or had he not placed his honour in his hands and in Carvalho's? He had. Then surely he could not suppose that they, his friends, would have left him wretchedly in the mire . . .

'But . . .' persisted Alves.

'But what? It is clear that you must fight. That is what was decided. There is no justification for pistols, for it was a mere flirtation. But since Senhor Machado has no right to flirt with your wife, there is every reason why it should be with swords, a simpler kind of duel ... We are to meet them soon, at my house at eight o'clock, and settle everything.'

'And we have little time to lose,' said Carvalho, taking out his watch, 'for it is half past six and we still have to dine. I am hungry ... '

So Alves invited them to dine with him. Moreover, he had assumed that they would turn up at dinner time and had given orders for a larger joint to be prepared.

'There won't be more than a bite of meat,' he said, 'but after all, during a campaign, anything suffices ... And we are at war!'

It was the first time he had smiled since the previous day. But the company of his friends at dinner made him happier, postponing the loneliness that he so dreaded.

And dinner was almost jolly. It had been agreed that they would not discuss the duel, nor the affair; but soon after the meat course, whenever Margarida was not there, they returned to the ruling topic, in brief phrases, vague allusions. In the end, Alves told the maid that she was not to come in again unless she heard the bell; and then the conversation did not flag. Alves described how he had got to know Ludovina, his courtship and his wedding day. Then he spoke about Machado, yet without rancour, even going so far as to say that he was a decent young fellow.

He himself used to go and fetch him from school when he was a youngster, and would sometimes take him to the theatre. And such memories touched him. He ended with a sob, begging them to talk no more on such matters. He rang the bell and Margarida brought in the joint. There was a brief silence. Medeiros praised the Colares wine. And Carvalho, referring to the Colares that he used to drink at Cape Verde, remembered a duelling case in which he had been a second. And as soon as the maid left the room, he recounted it; it was a case like that of Alves, also on account of a woman, but this one was black! To Medeiros, that seemed incredible, but Carvalho, a sparkle in his eye, praised black women:

'People who are accustomed to them want no one else… A black woman is a fine woman!'

'Deuce take it, let us not discuss women any further,' said Alves.

And in this plea, accompanied by a wan smile, there was a sort of resignation to his misfortune, an emergent idea of still enjoying life in the company of friends, the cares of business, without the vexations or complications which a passion for a skirt inevitably brings… Then they talked about Nunes Vidal.

In a situation like this, Medeiros was glad to have encountered Nunes, an upright young fellow, experienced and honourable. At first, he had feared that Machado intended to nominate as second that idiot Sigismondo that he went about with. And that brought Machado back into the conversation. Then, somewhat excited by the Colares, Medeiros confessed that he had 'fixed one' on Machado; he had been the lover of the French girl that Machado had been involved with. And he began to talk about himself, about his conquests. He returned to the story of the previous day when he had narrowly missed being caught in the kitchen ... Carvalho also had had such an experience in Tomar. On that occasion, he had been obliged to jump out of a window and had fallen into a hotbed ... Medeiros knew of a case much worse than that: a friend of his, Pinheiro, not the thin one but the other pock-marked one, had hidden in a pigsty for six hours. He had nearly died! And now, when he saw a pig, he turned as white as chalk.

Then, between Carvalho and Medeiros there was a whole string of anecdotes about infidelities. Only Alves, a faithful married man, had none of these stories. His life had been entirely domestic, without adventures; and he listened, sipping his coffee, enjoying this merry conclusion to the meal, smiling now and then.

And he ended up, feeling a warm breath of youthfulness and said:

'It is better that folk should amuse themselves at their own cost than at ours!'

Eight o'clock was approaching, and Carvalho began to put on his black gloves. Then Alves mentioned his accompanying them. He would stay in Medeiros's room, whilst they held their meeting in the lounge; that way, they would be spared the trouble of coming back to São Bento Street to report the outcome to him.

And although Medeiros considered that this would be contrary to etiquette, they finally agreed 'because it was not a very serious case!'

They ordered a carriage, and with all three of them crammed into the back of it, set off for the Estrela.

At Medeiros's house, the manservant had already lighted the candles in the chandelier and they had scarcely gone upstairs when the doorbell rang. It was the seconds, very punctual. And while Alves went and hid himself in the bedroom, the others went into the lounge, where the sound of voices soon began to rise.

In the darkness of the bedroom, not daring to summon the manservant, Alves hunted, groping along the table and the dressing-table, in search of a box of matches. He did not find them, but his fingers came into contact with a curtain; he drew it back and saw a chink of light through a door, from behind which came the sound of voices. On the other side was the lounge, where they were holding their meeting. He went nearer, but knocked over a jug, which rolled along, with the sound of water spilling. For a moment, he kept quite still and finally, paddling through the wet, went to put his ear to the keyhole.

In the lounge, there was silence, which he could not understand. At intervals, one of Machado's friends gave a cough. What the deuce were they up to? He tried to peep, but could only see, indistinctly, a bit of the mirror, in which the candlelight was reflected. The light suddenly disappeared, there was something dark in front of it, surely someone's back. Then a voice was raised, it was Medeiros's voice, and he was saying 'That seemed to him conclusive...' And at once there was the sound of other voices, mingled together, getting louder in a tumult which he could not make out. Finally, and quite distinctly, another voice was saying 'In such affairs, dignity is essential, above all else.'

Of course dignity was necessary, and it was not dignified for him to be there, eavesdropping at the door. Groping his way, he went back into the room and, after colliding with the sofa, sat down heavily. From the lounge, there was not a sound, an oppressive silence weighed upon the room. And that silence, that darkness, brought sombre thoughts of illness, of wounds. The following day, he perhaps would be in a darkened room, on a lonely bed, tended by Margarida... The idea caused him deep dismay.

He recalled stories that he had heard tell of wounds. At first, a sword wound would give only a feeling of coldness, the pain came afterwards, long-lasting during nights when the bedclothes grew hot and the body was unable to stir. And then he remembered all that Nunes Vidal had said to Carvalho – 'It was the first time that Machado had embraced her, in fun...' And what if that were really true? She too had told him, with a cry of anguish, that it was the first time!

It might very well have been a frolic, a piece of gallantry, what the English call a flirtation. Ought he to have forgiven it? Certainly not! Yet it was insufficient to justify a duel. It would have been enough to throw Machado out of the house... And other considerations occurred to him; Ludovina had never been more affectionate than of late. Previously, it had been himself who had had to take the lead, to arouse her. But recently, it was she who at times, without any prompting, had thrown her arms around his neck. Could he really say that she did not love him? No! and it was no pretence; he was no fool and well knew how to recognise genuine feeling. So why had she yielded to Machado's advances? Who could say? Coquetry, vanity... Anyway, the punishment was deserved. He would never see her again – and he would fight the man! Then he realised that he had never handled a sword, but Machado had given fencing lessons. He would be the one to be wounded, for certain! And dread returned. He thought he would not fear so greatly a quick death, a bullet through the heart... But a serious wound which would keep him in bed for weeks on end, his progress slow and feeble, inflammation, the risk of gangrene... It was horrible. His whole being shuddered at the thought... But it would end, honour demanded it!

Suddenly, in the corridor, he heard voices, laughter, the hearty sound of friends taking leave of each other. His heart beat faster, he was walking towards the door, when a light appeared. It was Medeiros, still holding the candle with which he had shown them out.

'Everything's settled,' said he, as he came in.

Behind him came Carvalho, who confirmed it: 'Everything has been settled.'

Pale and trembling, Alves looked at them.

'You are not going to fight,' said Medeiros, as he put the candlestick on the table.

'What did I tell you in the first place?' exclaimed Carvalho, beaming. 'Everything should stay as it was, that would be common sense.'

Then it was Medeiros who explained what had taken place. Nunes Vidal had behaved with extraordinary gentlemanliness. He had begun by saying that, if he had been convinced that there had been any betrayal on Machado's part, the crime of adultery with his partner's wife, he would not have become involved. He then said that if they insisted on the duel, they would be obliged to accept everything, without argument: the time, the place, the weapons. And having arrived at the chosen spot, Machado would have taken up his sword and allowed himself to be wounded, like a gentleman. But Nunes Vidal had appealed to them as men of honour and good sense.

'Wasn't that what he said, Carvalho?'

'And men of breeding,' Carvalho substituted.

'Exactly, and men of breeding. He appealed to us, asking whether we ought to agree to a duel when there was no justification for it and when, in a letter which Nunes gave us to read, Machado had declared, on his word of honour as a gentleman, that Senhora Ludovina was innocent, entirely innocent, and that nothing had been exchanged apart from some joking letters, and that embrace ... Well now, as Nunes Vidal had said, "What does a duel achieve? It compromises Senhora Ludovina, leads people to believe that there really has been misconduct, puts Senhor Alves into a ridiculous position, and damages the firm ... " '

'And Nunes's dilemma,' Carvalho reminded him.

'That's right, the dilemma,' said Medeiros, remembering. 'Nunes propounded this dilemma: the gentlemen demand swords. Very well, very well, but if there really had been misconduct, the sword is not enough; if not, it would be too much ... And in that way, we were agreed that there should be no duel ... '

Alves said not a word. But, in the silence, a feeling of peace and serenity was stealing over him. These important propositions of Nunes Vidal, such an honourable young man, almost convinced him that there had been nothing more than dalliance, with no serious intent. Nunes himself had said that if he had been convinced that there had been misconduct, he would not have become involved. Certainly not, for he was truly a gentleman. Well, if it had been mere dalliance, there was no reason to fight; and at that, he felt relieved. A thousand dreadful notions were disappearing and being replaced by others – of repose, tranquillity, perhaps even of happiness. To be sure, he would not forgive his wife even that simple dalliance; nor would he speak to Machado again. But if he could believe that they had not betrayed him, his life would be less bitter.

That consoled his self-esteem – for it would show that he was an upright and worthy husband, throwing out his wife merely for exchanging a glance. So his honour would remain secure and his feelings suffer less.

And he was filled with happiness at abandoning, putting aside, the violent ideas of death in which he had been involved, at entering once more into life's routine, his business, his relationships, his books. But then, at the thought of routine, of the business of his office, a thought occurred to him that filled him with disquiet:

'And Machado? I cannot speak to Machado again!'

Medeiros, however, had discussed this point with Nunes Vidal! And it was Nunes who had had a commonsense idea. Nunes had said that, from the moment when there was no more justification for a duel, there was no reason why they should break off their business relationship.

Alves protested: 'So is he to come into my office tomorrow?'

'Who says tomorrow, man? This is what Nunes Vidal said: tomorrow Machado writes you a formal letter, which the bookkeeper and the clerks may see, saying that he is going away with his mother, and asking you to keep an eye on his house, and so on ... Then, at the end of a month or two, he returns, you greet each other, each of you sits at his desk. You talk about what there is to discuss, about the business, and that's the end of it. You do not have intimate dealings, you even excuse yourselves from being on Christian-name terms.'

And as Alves stared at the floor, considering, the two of them came down on him in turn:

'That way, you stop everyone's mouth,' said Carvalho.

'You save yourself from ridicule,' said Medeiros.

'You save your wife from disrepute ... '

'You retain an intelligent and hard-working colleague ... '

'And perhaps a friend!'

Whereupon, tiredness overwhelmed Alves, his tension was relaxed. There came upon him an intense longing to think no more about this upset, to talk no more about it, to sleep in peace; and he yielded, gave up, asked in a trembling voice:

'Then, on your honour, you have decided that this way, everything turns out for the best?'

'We have!' they both replied.

Alves shook hands, first with one, then with the other, moved almost to tears:

'I've grateful, Carvalho! Thank you, Medeiros!'

And then, in order to shut people's mouths, the three of them went to the Public Promenade, where there were illuminations and a bonfire that evening, but they went first to have an ice cream at Martinho's.

8 ❧ FOR ALVES, A FRIGHTFUL EXISTENCE THEN BEGAN. Some weeks had passed and Machado had returned. Now, as of old, he occupied his desk in the office with the green repp.

During the time when Alves had been dreading this encounter, he had not thought it possible that they would ever again spend their days side by side, dealing with their papers, affected by a thousand common interests, still with the lively recollection of that July day. Yet, as it turned out, everything went off nicely and there were no disagreements.

On the eve of his return, Machado had written him a polite, almost humble, letter, in which a certain wistful touch was to be seen. He said he was about to return, would come into the office next day, that he hoped all thoughts of the past would disappear in their new relationship, which would always be governed by mutual respect. He went on to say that, while appreciating the awkwardness of the new solution, he was nevertheless accepting it only for a time, to maintain dignity and silence gossip, and reserving the right to leave the firm as soon as he could do so without scandal.

On the day, Alves went to the office earlier than usual and did a clever thing: he told the bookkeeper, in front of the cashier, that there had been disagreements between himself and Senhor Machado and that their relationship had undergone certain changes. These vague words were in fact intended to avoid surprise and comments on the part of the bookkeeper, now that he saw them facing each other—

distant, courteous, and addressing each other as Senhor Alves and Senhor Machado. The bookkeeper murmured that he quite understood – and a few moments later, Machado appeared. It was an awkward moment. For the rest of the day, they could scarcely attend to what they were doing, and Machado's slightest gesture – pulling out his handkerchief, taking a turn about the floor – awoke in Alves all sorts of disagreeable memories. Once or twice, he felt a violent urge to reproach him, blame him for all the unhappy things which now filled his life. But he restrained himself, almost unable to draw one breath after the other.

Machado's attitude was respectful and sad. They scarcely exchanged a word. A feeling of constraint weighed heavily on the atmosphere – and the stupid cashier made all this embarrassment more obvious by persisting in walking on tiptoe, as in a house where someone is dying.

Other days, all similar, succeeded each other; but, little by little, the presence of Machado ceased worrying Alves. He could already look at him without thinking of the yellow sofa…

A routine had become established: the last to come in courteously said good morning; and then, each in his armchair, they spoke only about business, with the fewest possible words. When there was nothing to do, Machado went out, leaving the office to Alves, who went on reading the newspapers, on the sofa. And things went on normally, without friction, because at bottom Machado had nothing but respect for Alves; and Alves, in spite of himself, still retained a store of sympathy for the boy that he had virtually educated. Soon, he was telling himself that, business apart, he was a pleasant rascal; the simple tone of his voice, his pleasant manners, attracted him irresistibly.

Thus it was that, when the first days of October arrived, all that tumultuous upset in Alves's life, which for weeks had taken hold of him like a sleep-walker, settled down. Ludovina was in Ericeira with her father, and the memory of the moment when he had seen her on the yellow sofa – the memory which had been like a raw wound in poor Alves's heart that the slightest movement, the least scratch, re-opened – was beginning to fade, leaving no more than one of those numb, vague, discomforts to which the body grows accustomed.

The disagreeable shock of the re-encounter with Machado had also passed. In the Gilders Street office, the routine of their personal relationship had been established – cool, courteous and tolerant.

And now, much calmer, Alves could see and feel with renewed intensity the circumstances of his life as a widower, which must be his for ever, and for the future he could foresee only discomfort and unhappiness.

At first, he had thought about leaving the house in São Bento Street, going to live in a hotel; but then he was afraid of public opinion, of gossip. No one knew that he had separated from his wife. It was supposed that she was at the seaside with her father and that Alves went to visit her from time to time; and he had to maintain this fiction by every means. Yet what was to be done about the two servants? He persisted with the idea of maintaining silence about his misfortune, keeping these two creatures under his control, bound to him by the self-interest of a pleasant situation. So he had stayed in São Bento and his life there was simply dreadful! One by one, the comforts he so much enjoyed had disappeared; for the two women, with no mistress to keep an eye on them, had got completely slack, realising that the master would not get rid of them, dependent as he was on their tongues.

For Alves, the discomfort of the day began at nine o'clock. It was a struggle to ensure that they brought him shaving water, and there was never any hot water. The cook, who now got up late, never had the stove going until ten o'clock. Then there was another struggle to get breakfast, and when it arrived, hurriedly and carelessly prepared, without any variety, it almost made him sick. Since August, boiled eggs had appeared before him every morning—now raw, now hard-boiled—and the same steaks, hard and black, like two pieces of burnt leather. He would sit down, look with disgust at the dirty napkin and feel deeply downcast. Where, alas!, was the time when Ludovina herself used to prepare his boiled eggs, using her little gold watch? There used then to be flowers always on the table, and his *Daily News* and *Journal of Commerce* beside his plate. He would open them with a feeling of peace and comfort, noticing around him the sound of her dress, the warmth of her presence, and a faint scent of toilet water.

Now, when he got home at four o'clock, he found the remains of his mournful breakfast still on the table, scraps of meat on his plate, dregs at the bottom of his teacup, everything filthy and miserable, with flies circling all over it. There were always crumbs on the floor. Every day, something got broken. And at the month's end there were colossal bills, wastefulness, an absurd piling up of expense. Twice already, he had met men on the stairs, callers for the maids. His dirty linen lay about in corners, and when he became angry and burst into the kitchen, shouting, exploding, the two creatures made no reply, pretended to be concerned, even more hateful than an insolent answer. They lowered their heads respectfully, made a stupid apology, and then stayed there, smirking and sipping glasses of wine.

But worst of all were the lonely evenings. He had always been a home-loving man, fond of coming home early, putting on his slippers, enjoying his own domestic scene. In the old days, Ludovina would play the piano in the drawing-room for a while; he would go round and light the lamps, like a devotee preparing an altar, for he loved music and he would finish his cigar in his armchair, listening to her playing, gazing at the mass of her dark hair hanging over her shoulders in graceful abandon and intimacy. Certain pieces that she played gave him a feeling of having his heart caressed by something soft and velvety, and made him swoon; one especially, a certain waltz, *Souvenir of Andalusia*... How long it had been since he had heard it played!

While the summer lasted, he went for a walk every evening. But even the sight of the streets revived memories of lost happiness. There would be an open balcony, with a young woman in a bright dress, enjoying the air, and this made him think of his lonely house, now lacking the swirl of a woman's skirts; and at nightfall, there was a window which revealed the subdued light of a pleasant evening party, and coming from it the gentle sound of a piano... And worn out, his shoes dusty, he then felt acutely the unhappy evidence of his loneliness.

The worst evenings were those when he sought the liveliness of the Public Promenade. It was dread of loneliness that took him there; but the feeling of isolation in the midst of so many people, beneath the illuminated trees, seeing so many men each with a woman on his arm, proved even more miserable than the chilly, deserted drawing-room, with the neglected piano!

Later on, when winter was beginning, matters became intolerable. November was very wet. He would come back late from the office and after hastily swallowing a boring dinner, would hang about, his feet in slippers, as he wandered in boredom from room to room. No armchair, however comfortable, gave him a feeling of rest and well-being: his precious books seemed to have lost all their interest, because he no longer felt her at his side, sewing while he was reading, under the same light. And shyness, unease, a vague sense of shame, prevented him from going to the theatre.

And now he always felt restless, for she had returned from Ericeira and he knew she was there, in the same street, ten minutes walk from the house in which he was enduring all the sorrows of widowerhood. Twenty times a night he would mentally make the journey, climb Neto's stairs, penetrate into the familiar room, its chaise-longue covered in red cretonne. It was in that chaise-longue that she used to stretch out when they went to visit his father-in-law. And envy, despair, came over him at the thought of her there, sitting with some needlework or a book in her hands, peaceful, without a thought for him.

On returning from Ericeira, Neto had come to see him. And the rogue's every word had been a stab for Alves. They had had a fine time in Ericeira. They had seen no one, for after all, Ludovina's situation did not allow of entertainments or picnics, but they had spent a very nice time together, as a family. Ludovina had bathed, she was well, had put on weight, and he had never seen her look so attractive; she had devoted herself to the piano and seemed placid and good-humoured. And after picturing her thus, so healthy, so attractive, Neto had gone away, without uttering the words which Alves was longing to hear—a simple phrase, 'Make it up!'

For that was now his ardent wish. Yet, out of pride, dignity, a touch of jealousy and ill-humour, he did not want to take the first step. In his view, it was for Neto to bring about this reconciliation–and he now began to loathe him, perceiving that he wanted to keep his daughter at home. It was easy to understand why; in no way did the rogue object to the thirty milreis which fell into his purse each month. Alves even thought about withdrawing the allowance from her, but a sense of chivalry prevented him from doing that.

What tortured him above everything was not yet having been able to see her. In vain did he walk to and fro in front of Neto's house; in vain, on Sundays, did he go to mass at her church; in vain did he hang around the house of her dressmaker, a certain Dona Justina in the square at Carmo, in the hope of seeing her coming out or going in. He did not see her until two days before Christmas when, as he was leaving a tobacconist's and lighting his cigar, he caught sight of her from behind ...

He was so upset, so agitated that instead of hurrying to catch up with her and see her, as his longing insistently demanded, he quickly hid at the back of the shop and stayed there, hesitant, pale and benumbed, his heart pounding. To see her again was all he wanted, but when he recovered and went to look for her again, he went vainly up and down the Chiado, without seeing her–he had lost her. So he went home, deeply depressed, having in his mind's eye throughout the evening that upright figure, dressed in black, with a yellow flower in her hat.

Yet the spell had been broken, and a week later, when he

was going down the Post Office steps, he saw her with her sister, coming up. There was the same perturbation, the same embarrassment, the same absurd impulse to hide in a doorway...But in the end, with pounding heart, he decided to face up to the encounter; he quickened his step, clenched his fists, drew himself up. And as he trembled, out of the corner of his eye, he saw her lower her gaze and blush in confusion.

He went home in a state of extraordinary excitement. He felt that he adored her, and his heart fluttered at the delightful idea of holding her in his arms again. Yet, at the same time, he felt a furious, indefinable sense of jealousy, jealousy of other men in the street, of the walks she took, of the words she might say, the glances she might give, to other people. He wanted her with him there, under lock and key, within those walls which were his own—in his home, imprisoned in his arms. And quite unable to stay indoors, he went out, almost at midnight, and went to stare at Neto's windows.

When he came back, he wrote her an absurd letter, six passionate pages, interspersed with reproaches. But on reading it through, he found it too wordy, not affectionate enough, and tore it up.

That night, he did not sleep. He constantly saw her beautiful face, glowing, her long eyelashes lowered...Yes, as Neto had said, she was plumper, more handsome. Oh! what a divine woman. And she was his, his wife! Positively, that miserable, solitary life could not continue!

January passed without his seeing her again—and his passion grew. He was awaiting some chance that would bring them together. Each morning, he imagined that the day would not pass without their meeting, and he was determined to speak to her.

Once already, on meeting Neto, he had referred vaguely to the inconvenience of their separation. But Neto merely shrugged his shoulders, with an air of despondency and paternal suffering. It was very sad, but what was there to be done? Then, one evening in the Martinho, Neto stopped to speak to him again. He said he had been thinking things over and that he felt disposed to take a trip to Minho with his daughter... to avoid gossip! Alves was aghast and burst out:

'But it won't be at my expense!'

And turning his back on him, he went home, furious. It was seven o'clock and there was a clear cold moon. He was nearing his door when, on the pavement, he came face to face with Ludovina, who was returning home, accompanied by her sister. Instinctively, he stepped quickly off the pavement, but stopped and with a sudden impulse, turned and called out 'Ludovina!' She stopped in amazement. They were near a grocer's shop, in the lamplight, and went on looking at each other, their faces flushed and, in their confusion, not finding a word to say. Alves was so bemused that he did not greet his sister-in-law, did not even see her. And his first words were absurd:

'Well, they say that you are going to Minho!'

Ludovina, perplexed, looked at him and turned to her sister.

'To Minho?' she murmured.

And in a choking voice he said:

'Your father told me ... I thought it a most ridiculous idea! Oh! Teresa, forgive me for not seeing you ... Have things been going well with you? And you, Ludovina, have you been all right?'

She shrugged her shoulders: 'So, so ...'

With a look, he devoured her, finding her adorable in a velvet cape which he did not recognise and which must be new.

'It seems that you enjoyed yourself very much at Ericeira.'

She smiled wryly: 'I? Well!' and she added with a little sigh: 'I am bored and unhappy ...'

Tenderness, great pity, overcame him; and, near tears, in a quavering voice, he stammered:

'There, there ...'

Then he said casually, but already in an intimate tone, as if from that moment their reconciliation was complete:

'Well, things are not going well at home ... Margarida has been very neglectful. And there's something I wanted to ask you ... How the deuce do I light the reading-lamp, which I have not been able to put in order?'

She laughed, Teresa also. They knew very well that from now on, Ludovina was once again Godofredo's wife. She said:

'If you like, I will come and teach Margarida how to do it.'

His whole being gave a cry of happiness:

'Do come, do! Teresa can come, too. It will only take a moment.'

And he led the way in, climbed the staircase, opened the door, overcome with pleasure at hearing the swish of her dress going up the stairs.

Hearing voices, Margarida had come running, and when she saw the ladies, she was dumbfounded.

'Bring me the reading-lamp from the study,' he said to her.

Ludovina and her sister had gone into the dining-room and had remained standing, their hats on and their hands in their muffs, while Godofredo, just like a child, rushed into the kitchen, then went into the bedroom, hastened to light the candles in the lounge, where there was no gas. Meanwhile, Ludovina was examining the dining-room, the sideboard, the carpet, scandalised by the neglect that she found there—stopping to look at a beautiful cut-glass fruit bowl which had a broken handle. Alves had come home and found it like that.

'Alas!' he exclaimed. 'Everywhere there is destruction such as you cannot imagine. Look, come in here, come and see, come here into our bedroom...'

He went in, she followed, blushing like a bride going into her wedding chamber; and she was scarcely inside before he seized her, pulled her towards the wash-basin recess, and there in the shadow kissed her violently, wildly, on her eyes, her hair, even her hat, enjoying the sweetness of her skin, feeling faint from the touch of the freshness she had brought in from the chill of the street.

Quietly, she said:

'No, no! Teresa is looking! . . .'

'Send her away, I will go and take her,' he murmured. 'You, my love, stay, never let us part again . . .'

And with a kiss, she gave her consent.

9 🦶 THE FOLLOWING DAY, IN A SENTIMENTAL MOMENT, the weather being magnificent and Alves wanting to give his happy state a more poetic environment, he suggested that they should go and spend a few days at Sintra. It was a second honeymoon. They stayed at the Lawrence, had a small sitting-room to themselves. They got up late, drank champagne at dinner and kissed each other furtively on benches beneath the trees. Godofredo did not leave Ludovina for a moment, eager to enjoy once again the intimacy that he thought he had lost, feeling unbounded delight at seeing her dressing, finding her negligee on a chair, or helping her to do her hair.

After four days, they returned home, continued their honeymoon in Lisbon without a cloud, and with no thought of expense, hired a carriage and a box at the San Carlos. Godofredo was anxious to be seen with her everywhere, so as to shut people's mouths. At the San Carlos, he would take a prominent box, making a display of his domestic happiness.

And as Ludovina had returned from the Ericeira air more robust and content, magnificent in the beauty of a fine brunette, men in the stalls stared at her, and a pair of opera glasses was invariably focused on her.

'They are staring,' said Alves. 'They are surprised to see us together ... well, this is to let them know.'

And he slowly drew back his hands from the front of the box, smiling at his Lulu.

On one of these evenings, the *Africana* was being given its first performance, and Ludovina, who throughout the performance had been tortured by a new pair of shoes, was anxious to leave in the middle of the fifth act. He at once agreed, notwithstanding his enjoyment of Alteroni's tragic singing, beneath the branches of the manchineel tree, in the tragic light of the full moon. He shepherded her out, gave her his arm, and beneath the entrance portico they were waiting for the carriage when suddenly Machado appeared, a cigar between his teeth. Obviously, he had not seen them, for he continued across the entrance, with his slightly swaying gait, fastening his white scarf and buttoning up his coat. Suddenly, he came face to face with them. For a moment, he seemed to hesitate – confused, pale, his fingers absent-mindedly fumbling with the buttons. Then, very formally, he doffed his hat. Under the high hood of her white cape, she nodded slightly, lowering her gaze, solemn, impassive and unmoving, with her long blue train gathered into her hand. After a moment's hesitation, Alves finally called out quite loudly:

'Hello, Machado, good night to you!'

Machado went quickly away.

Next day, when Alves reached the office, Machado was already at his desk. After the usual laconic greetings, Alves went on sorting over his papers, reading the correspondence. Then he glaced casually, abstractedly, at the newspaper. He seemed preoccupied, his mind on something else, and suddenly he leaned back, snapped his fingers and asked Machado:

'Well, how did Alteroni strike you yesterday?'

It was the first time that he had spoken to him about anything unconnected with the business of the firm! Machado stood up to reply, rather nervously:

'I liked him very much ... And ... '

'A fine voice, eh?'

And those commonplace words, as soon as they were uttered, were like opening the floodgates of a dike. Alves also stood up, and there was a torrent of words between them, hesitant at first, then warming, getting close to each other again, a lively current of mutual feeling. They were like two friends meeting after a long absence, and each of them recognised in the other what he had always esteemed in him. At a quip by Machado about the tenor, Alves burst out laughing, and a remark by Alves about the playing of the violins greatly interested Machado, making him think that Alves was really fond of listening to music.

Alves then talked about their visit to Sintra; and for a while they chatted about Sintra, each mentioning his favourite places there, the impression they had made on him, as though they felt the need, after that long separation, to compare their respective thoughts and tastes.

Then, as Machado had to go off early, their handshake on taking leave of each other was deeply felt, warm, a complete reconciliation, uniting them again for ever!

So Alves's life became serene and happy once more. At São Bento Street, order and happiness were restored; at breakfast, there were no more raw or hard-boiled eggs, and already in the evenings the *Souvenir of Andalusia* restored to Godofredo his dreamlike, happy impression of the gardens of Granada; and all the time, her voice, the swish of her dress, flooded his heart with happiness.

And so the winter had gone by, spring had passed and they were in the first days of March when, as Alves was leaving one morning, he saw Margarida in the corridor, between the two doors, surreptitiously, secretly, handing a letter to Ludovina. It was as though a stone had struck him in the chest. He could scarcely cope with the door catch; at once, he imagined another man, another lover, and his happiness, the happiness that had been so laboriously rebuilt, collapsed again. He felt an absurd sense of panic, as if he were the victim of fate, of a terrible and beastly destiny, the fateful inconstancy of women.

He thought that it might be Machado again, and a surge of blood passed before his eyes, he swore that this time there would be no meetings, no consultations, no seconds—he would go into the office and put a bullet point blank into his heart.

And he felt so upset that he could not bear the sight of Machado; he did not go to the office; he wandered around the Baixa, with that vision of the maid's hand, the white paper, Ludovina's embarrassed look, ever before his eyes. He went home, sombrely and silently, could not settle down, but went from room to room, slamming the doors, like a man suffocating, feeling the very air around him charged with deceit and treachery. Ludovina, alarmed, at last asked what was the matter.

'It's nerves,' was his unmannerly reply. But a moment later, yielding to a violent impulse, he turned on her, declared that he had had enough of mysteries, that life was hell, and that he wanted to know what was the paper that Margarida had passed to her.

She stared at him, astonished by his violence, that strident voice, and her hand instinctively sought the pocket of her house coat. He followed her gesture:

'Ah! you have the letter there! Let me see it.'

Then she showed that she was offended by such distrust — were the suspicions, the questions, starting again? So could she not receive a piece of paper without his wanting to poke his nose in?

Pale, with fists clenched, he shouted:

'Either you give me the letter or I will do you an injury!'

She turned very pale, called him a villain and, weeping, fell on to the sofa, her face in her hands.

'Give me the letter!' he shouted, standing on tiptoe. 'Give me the letter... And this time must not be like the last... You'll go into a convent!... I'll kill you!'

And he did not wait for her reply; he threw himself upon her, twisted her arm, tore the pocket of her dress, seized the letter. But he could not decipher the writing, it was a misspelt scribble on a piece of ruled paper. It began: 'My dear Madam', was signed 'Maria do Carmo' and referred to almsgiving, to the little one who was recovering from measles, and to the prayers that they had never ceased to offer for that blessed charity...

Trembling, wretched, humiliated, with the piece of paper in his hand, he came and sat down beside Ludovina, who was weeping, with her face in her hands. And putting his arm round her waist, he stammered:

'There now, I see that it was nothing... Forgive me, tell me what it is!'

She pushed him away, rose to her feet, greatly offended. Was he satisfied? Had he read the letter, then? It was from a man, was it?

Ashamed, he stammered:

'But why all this mystery?'

And as she wiped her eyes, choking back her sobs, lovely as she stood there, he did not hold back, but felt the need to humble himself, fell on his knees, and with his hands clasped together, murmured:

'Forgive me, little Lulu, it was my stupidity...'

With another, even greater sob, she pressed her fingers to her face. Then, almost weeping himself, he kissed her hands, clasped her knees, then ended by getting up with an effort, clutching her dress and covering her throat with kisses.

And then, in their mutual distress, between embraces, she told him about the alms which she had secretly been giving. It was to a poor girl she had befriended in Ericeira, whom a villain had seduced and abandoned with her two children, one still at the breast.

'But why did you make a mystery of it, my love?' he persisted, moved and very affectionate.

Then she confessed that she had already given the girl more than five milreis and was fearful lest he might consider that extravagant. So great was Godofredo's happiness that he said:

'Extravagance! Give her another five...That is what I intend.'

And it all ended with a kiss.

Only then did Alves feel ashamed of his morning suspicions and his anger against Machado; he had even thought once more of killing him! And now he felt the need to see him again, to shake his hand warmly—feeling at this moment an even greater friendliness towards him, moved by a feeling of gratitude.

Next day, when he came into the office, Alves did not hold back but, for no apparent reason, put his arm around

Machado, who returned his partner's embrace, not finding his effusiveness at all strange, but, to Alves's surprise, gently and sadly. And his astonishment increased when he found that Machado's eyes were red, as though he had been weeping.

'It is my mother, who is very ill,' said Machado, in answer to his partner's inquiry.

And Alves, his own happiness interrupted by this bad news, could only murmur:

'That's dreadful!'

Yes, things were bad. And the doctor held out no hope. The poor lady suffered from a complex of illnesses, liver, kidneys and heart, which seemed now to be resulting in a complete breakdown of her health. The previous evening, she had had an attack lasting two hours. He thought she had died, but in the morning had been greatly relieved to find that he had been mistaken.

Poor Machado sighed as he recounted this. His affection for his mother had always been his strongest emotion. They had always lived together and on her account he had never wanted to marry. Now all this loss seemed to take away from his life everything that had made it dear.

'God cannot want such a disaster,' murmured Alves, greatly upset.

Machado shrugged his shoulders resignedly, and soon afterwards went to return to the side of the poor sufferer.

Now, three or four times every day, Alves went to

Machado's home to get news. The poor lady was getting worse. Happily, she did not feel any pain – and her last days were comforted by the love with which her son surrounded her, not stirring from her bedside for a moment, subduing his grief, hiding his paleness, cheering her up, talking of plans and trips into the country, and even joking, as in happier times.

Then, one evening, Alves stopped by for news. The maid answered, with her apron to her eyes: the mistress had died an hour earlier, like a little bird. He went in. And Machado threw himself into his arms, overwhelmed with grief.

Alves did not leave him, but spent the night there. He looked after the funeral arrangements, the invitations, the purchase of a grave on St John's Hill. And on the following day, in the solemnity of condolence calls, friends of the family shook hands with him as warmly, silently, as they did with Machado himself, recognising in him more than a friend, almost a brother.

The funeral was well attended; there were more than twenty carriages. Alves carried the key of the casket and took charge of the arrangements at the cemetery, invited the closest friends to be pall bearers, talked with the priests, did not spare himself; and when the coffin was lowered into the grave, his tears went with it.

Next day, Machado went away to Vila Franca, to the home of an aunt, and Alves took him to the station, looked after his baggage and again wept as he embraced him.

A fortnight later, Machado returned. Again he occupied

his desk in the office with the green repp. But he did not seem the same. He was calmer, but so sad in his mourning that Alves, always a romantic, wondered to himself whether those lips would ever smile again.

Later, seeing that he was staying at his desk and reluctant to go home to the now empty house, to the now solitary dinner, he had one of his sudden kindly impulses: he forgot it all, opened his arms to Machado:

'Well, what will be, will be. Come and have dinner with us!'

And he did not let him hold back; he put on his coat, almost pushed him down the steps, called a cab, thrust him into it, and took him triumphantly to São Bento Street.

During the journey, Machado said nothing, fearing the encounter, already growing pale, searching for something normal to say to Ludovina.

On the staircase, they heard at once the sound of the piano and a few moments later, putting his head round the drawing-room curtain, Alves, beaming, exclaimed:

'Ludovina, I have brought you a guest!'

She rose and suddenly found herself face to face with Machado, who bowed deeply, hiding his confusion in that act of elaborate courtesy.

She blushed, but her voice was clear and firm as she held out her hand to him, saying:

'How do you do, Senhor Machado? Have things been going well with you?'

He stammered a few words and remained standing, slowly rubbing his hands. while Ludovina tried to dispel his embarrassment with a torrent of words, telling Godofredo about a visit she had had from the Medonças, talking about Senhor Medonça and the Medonça boy, vivaciously, nervously, her ears burning. Then she hurried out of the room to give instructions.

When they were left alone, Alves made this profound remark:

'So, when one is well brought up, everything turns out right.'

Shortly afterwards, she came back, more at ease, having no doubt put a touch of powder on her face. Machado was sitting on the famous yellow sofa and made to get up, to offer her his seat. But she did not accept it, sat down alongside him in an armchair, and as though she wanted to make amends for something she had overlooked, hastened to say, with a sigh:

'Senhor Machado, I felt your loss very much...'

He bowed, murmuring a few words, and Alves intervened, saying:

'Let us not talk about that now! One must accept God's decisions: it is past!'

But a shadow had come over Machado's sensitive face and a mournful air of depression hung heavily on the room. Yet it was this very sadness which suddenly put them at their ease. It was as though Machado, in his deep mourning, thinking about his mother, the still fresh grave, was not the man who had drunk glasses of port with his arm around her, there on the yellow sofa. It was another Machado, a serious young man hurt by suffering, who needed to be consoled, who had grown older and for ever averse to amorous adventures.

She found him changed, and as she looked at him, could scarcely remember what he had been like before. He, too, found her so different that it might have been his first visit to the house.

The husband had forgiven. They too would forgive. And they ended by looking each other in the face, speaking naturally, without embarrassment, she saying 'Senhor Machado', he replying formally, both of them cool, having ceased for ever to tremble before each other, like two burntout cinders.

And the dinner was peaceful, calm, intimate, almost jolly.

So life went on unfolding, uneventful and smooth, as it really is. Machado's period of mourning ended. He began again to go to theatres, had other Spanish girls, courted other ladies. Then Neto died suddenly of apoplexy, in an omnibus, and Teresa came to live with her sister.

After two years, Machado married a girl named Cantanhede, for whom he had conceived an absurd, wild infatuation that would not wait and which led him to complete his courtship, betrothal and marriage, all within the space of a month. There was a ball, Ludovina appeared in a beautiful gown, but she did not dance.

Then at the end of a year, poor Cantanhede died in

childbirth and again, overwhelmed with grief, Machado wept in Alves's arms. Again Alves took the key of the casket, and gave long silent handshakes during the visits of condolence. But this time, Ludovina helped him, weeping too, because she and Cantanhede had been close friends, accustomed to spend their days together, never apart; and her grief was almost as great as the unhappy Machado's. Again life went on, smooth and uneventful, as is its wont. And at the end of two years, Machado fell in love with an actress from the Ginasio. At this time, there was an upheaval in the Alves household, the marriage of Teresa — against the wishes of her sister and brother-in-law — to a clerk from the Customs, an insignificant nitwit, without a penny, who had bewitched the girl because he was fair, as blond as an ear of corn. They had to be married, because Teresa was wasting away, threatening to throw herself from a window — and there were other suspicions.

The months went by and then the years. The business of Alves & Co. expanded, became more prosperous. The office, now more spacious, more luxurious, with six clerks, was at the corner of Silver Street. Alves was balder, Ludovina had grown stouter. They kept a carriage, and in summer went to Sintra.

Then Machado got married again, to a widow — an inexplicable marriage, for the widow was neither handsome nor wealthy; but she did have remarkable eyes, very dark, with long eyelashes, very tremulous, ready to die with languor.

It was a quiet wedding and the newly-weds set off for Paris. They returned, came to live quite near to the Alveses, who had now moved to a villa at Buenos Aires. And another close friendship developed between Ludovina and the lady with the languorous eyes. Very soon, Ludovina became the slave of this strange creature, who also enslaved Machado, had a strong influence over Alves, and dominated all around her—servants, relatives, tradesmen—effortlessly, with her air of superiority, her chubby figure, and her languorous eyes with long eyelashes.

Now, the two families live next door to each other and are growing old side by side. On Ludovina's birthday, there is always a grand ball and always, inseparable from this day, there comes back to Alves the memory of that other anniversary, when he came home and saw on the yellow sofa ... But what an age since that happened!

And now the memory merely makes him smile. But it also makes him think; for that incident remains the outstanding event of his life, and from it he draws his general philosophy and his normal reflections. As he often says to Machado, what a wise thing is prudence!

If, on the day of the yellow sofa, he had given way to his rage, or if he had persisted later in thoughts of rancour and revenge, what would his life have been like? He would even now be parted from his wife, his close business association with his partner would have been broken off, his firm would not have prospered, nor his fortune increased; and his private

The Yellow Sofa 111

life might have been that of a sour bachelor, dependent on maidservants, perhaps besmirched by licentiousness.

In the long years that had gone by, how many fine things he would have lost, how many domestic pleasures, how many comforts, how many pleasant family evenings, how many of the satisfactions of friendship, how many long days of peace and honour! By this time, he would be old, irritable, his life ruined, his health destroyed, with that shame from the past for ever burning him up.

And how differently it had turned out!

He had held out his arms in compassion to a guilty wife, to a disloyal friend; and with that simple embrace, he had made his wife for ever an ideal partner and his friend the soul of loyalty.

And now there they were, all together side by side, respected, serene, happy, growing old in comradeship, in the midst of prosperity and peace.

Sometimes, as he thought about it all, Alves could not help smiling with satisfaction. Then he would slap his friend on the back, remind him of the past, say to him with a smile:

'And we were on the point of fighting each other! Young people are always rash – and all because of a joke, Machado, my friend!'

And the other one, smiling too, would slap him on the back and reply:

'All on account of a big joke, Alves, my friend!'